Halloween In New Orleans with A Mama's Boy

Bestselling Author: O'sharra

"Justin please don't leave me. I promise I will do better. I know we don't do the things we used to do, but how can you blame a mother for loving her child? It was hard for us to conceive so when we adopted him, I felt like God had finally given us a second chance at being parents. He means everything to me," Stephanie cried to her husband Justin.

"He isn't even biologically our child. The only reason I went along with it was because you were obsessed with the thought of having a child. Maybe it wasn't in God's will for us to be parents, and that's why we weren't able to conceive naturally. Have you ever thought about that?" Justin yelled at his wife. When she had brought the idea of adopting a child to him, he was against it from the beginning. She wouldn't stop bitching about it, so eventually he conceded with her demands and after months of background checks, counseling, and thirty thousand dollars, they finally had an infant son. When they had first brought the baby home, Justin noticed an immediate change in his wife, she had gone from fucking him, and sucking his dick every night to barely once a week. All she did was run back and forth when the baby cried. Stephanie wasn't the same woman he had fallen in love with. She no longer cared about going to the salon to get her hair pressed, getting her nails and feet done, or buying sexy clothes to look good for him. All she cared about was that damned child, and Justin was over it.

"How could you say something like that Justin, he's just a baby. We are all he has," Stephanie replied. Duevon began to cry loudly in his crib. Stephanie jumped from her seat and ran to the other room to pick him up.

Justin shook his head in disgust. Here he was with his suitcase lying on the bed, and preparing to leave her. She couldn't even let the little bastard cry for a few minutes so they could have a discussion. He walked over to the bathroom and grabbed his toiletry bag so that he could throw his toothbrush, shaving kit, and deodorant into it. He walked quickly from the master bath and back into the bedroom. He already knew exactly where he was going. There was a girl at work that he had been cheating on Stephanie with for two months. The more time he spent with her at her place, the more he realized that the peace and quiet was what he preferred. She didn't have kids, nor did she want them. The days when he lied to his wife about going on work trips, he and his mistress would lay up in her house in peace. From sun-up to sun-down, they fucked like teenagers, binge watched movies, and went to bars in the late hours of the night. He loved the freedom that came with not having children. This was the freedom that he and Stephanie used to have before they adopted Duevon. He was tired of this boring ass lifestyle, and he planned to go to the courthouse and file for a divorce first thing Monday morning. Stephanie could give all of her love and attention to Duevon. Justin was sick of fighting and competing for her attention.

He grabbed his bag and walked out of the bedroom door, just as Stephanie was coming out of their son's nursery rocking him in her arms.

"Baby please, don't do this. I'm your wife, and this is your son. You can't walk out on your family like this," she begged.

"I'll stay, under one condition. Send that screaming ass kid back to the adoption agency and let's go back to living our lives with just us two. He's been here for three months and all he does is cry, hog all of your attention, and shit every five minutes. Do you notice that we never have fun anymore? You are only twenty-one years old, and I just turned Twenty- five. Sure, we got married young, but I miss the way we used to be. We don't need kids because everyone else has them. Fuck what other people are doing, let's live our lives the way we want." Justin made one last pleading attempt with his wife as he sat his suitcase at his feet.

"How could you ask me to just return him like he's a pair of shoes Justin? I'm not doing that. Fuck you and that bitch who you are leaving me for. I know it's another woman, I just looked over your cheating ass ways because I love you so much. Get the fuck out!" Stephanie yelled at the top of her lungs causing Duevon to cry again. Justin laughed while shaking his head.

He picked up his bag and walked down the stairs, "Good luck!" He shouted behind him as he slammed the door hard leaving Stephanie and her child standing in the middle of the floor.

"It's ok little one, mama's here." Stephanie cooed as she rocked her baby back and forth to calm him.

"We are all we have and all we need." She cried to him as she paced the floor for hours until he eventually fell asleep. Taking him to her bedroom, she laid him next to her in the bed and wrapped her arms around his small body lovingly.

"All we have and all we need."

Halloween In New Orleans with A Mama's Boy

"I asked God to send me a man who would always love me, so he gave me a son"
-Stephanie Howell

Chapter One

October 2022

"MMMHMMMMMM, YES DADDYYY!" The groupie screamed out as Duevon fucked her roughly from the back. The only sounds that filled the room was the sound of skin slapping as his pelvis pounded her fat ass. Even though he had been fucking her for weeks, he didn't know her real name; nor did he care to find out. He slapped her on her ass like he was punishing her for being the bad girl that she was. He then wrapped her thirty-inch weave around his fist and yanked her hair like he was trying to snatch her frontal loose.

"I LOOVEEEE YOU NUMBER 13," She moaned out his jersey number causing him to grin.

For three years, Duevon Howell had been the corner back for the New Orleans Saints. He didn't get as much shine as Winston or Dalton, but he had signed a hefty contract for a quarter of a million dollars, so he didn't give a fuck about being a household name. All he cared about was being in the league and getting as much pussy as his twenty-four-year-old body would allow him to.

"I'M CUMMMINNNN'!" She screamed loudly, right before Stephanie Howell busted into the room.

"DUEVON MICHEAL HOWELL, WHAT DID I TELL YOU ABOUT FUCKING THESE GROUPIE HOES?" His mother shouted as she stormed into his hotel room like an angry wife catching her husband in the middle of an unfaithful act.

"AARRGHHH!" The girl screamed loudly as she rushed to

cover her naked body underneath the duvet.

"MAMA!" Duevon screamed out angrily as he placed his hands in front of his dick to hide his nakedness from Stephanie.

"Boy, I have seen your dick a million times. I used to wipe your ass remember?" She told him as her red bottoms clanked loudly on the hardwood floors. She walked over to the bed, grabbed the girl by her hair, and dragged her from underneath the covers.

"LET ME GO, YOU CRAZY BITCH!" The girl screamed as she tried to fight his mother off her petite body. The biggest thing on her was her ass, and that was exactly the way Duevon loved his women.

"SHUT UP HOE!" His mother retorted nonchalantly as she dragged the girl out of the room and tossed her out the door like trash.

"Stedman, get rid of her!" She yelled out to Duevon's bodyguard who had been standing on the outside of his door while he handled his business. His mother had hired Stedman, and Duevon knew it was more to watch him and report his whereabouts more than his safety.

"Can a nigga get some privacy?" He asked Stephanie angrily as he stood to his feet and grabbed his Versace underwear. He was so annoyed with his mother constantly barging in on him and running away the only peace he had, he was a grown ass man and couldn't even catch a nut without her breathing down his neck.

"You aren't even going to wash your dick after letting that skank bounce all on it?" She asked him while sitting down on the unmade bed and looking down at her full set of long stiletto nails to make sure she hadn't broken one.

"WAIT ONE DAMN MINUTE!" She yelled out as she jumped from the bed and walked over to Duevon. She snatched the front of his briefs down exposing his once hard dick. "YOU ARE OUT HERE FUCKING THESE GROUPIE HOES RAW? HOW STUPID COULD YOU

BE DUEVON?" She asked him angrily while smacking him upside his head.

"Chill ma, I was going to make the hoe take a Plan B pill and watch her swallow it." He looked to the sky in aggravation. He knew that his mother was more concerned about a bitch popping up pregnant and coming after his earnings, than she was about him catching an incurable sexually transmitted disease.

"I told you, even though you make them take Plan B's you can't just be out here fucking these hoes raw. They are slick. They can hide the pill under their tongue and pretend to swallow it! Haven't you learned anything from what Brittany did to PJ? Are you trying to become some ambitionless slut's meal ticket?" She questioned him as she walked over to the mini bar and grabbed one of the little shots from the hotel suite's refrigerator.

Duevon took a deep breath and placed his hand over his face like he was four years old.

"Well, I didn't even nut, so unless the bitch is the Virgin Mary, there won't be any little Duevon's running around here to make your fine ass a grandma anytime soon," he laughed loudly.

Stephanie smirked and threw her long human weave over her shoulder. The hair rested on top of her ass that he had paid good money to get enhanced by the best doctor in Beverly Hills.

"Don't even speak that out of your damn mouth," she told him while rolling her eyes.

"Now come on and take your mother out to brunch! I have been fiending for some of that lobster from the upscale place downtown and I want to do some shopping. Make sure you wash that whore's cum from your dick." She told him nonchalantly as she turned to walk out of the room and slammed the door loudly behind her.

Duevon shook his head and went to take a shower. "Women." He said to himself as he took his underwear off and stepped into a scalding hot shower. This was the third time this week his mother had barged in on him while he was trying to handle his business. Practice was grueling enough, and the only places he found peace were the bottom of a bottle of liquor or inside some pussy. He knew that he had to be smarter if he wanted to hide his next piece of ass from his overbearing mother. He would have to duck Stedman's snitching ass and pay for the next hotel room in cash so she couldn't check his account to see what hotel he was at. It was a shame that he was single, and he had to move like a married man just to get some ass.

A few hours later, they laughed loudly over lobster and bottomless mimosas.

"Don't eat another piece of that steak, because you have practice tomorrow." Stephanie scolded him as she took a sip from her champagne flute.

"Ok Kris Jenner." He told her sarcastically as he cut into the juicy T-bone steak and placed it in his mouth. To spite her, he licked the fork sexually as if he were pleasing a woman. A lot of people thought that his relationship with Stephanie was borderline inappropriate but neither one of them gave a damn what people thought. He could be himself around her and she would laugh loudly and be completely unbothered.

"That fork better be the only thing you are licking on, don't be out here putting these little hoes pussy in your mouth." She retorted while waving her hand at his silly antics.

"I was just about to do that before you busted up in the room like one of those real housewives." He joked with her causing her to laugh.

"Was there anything else I can get for you all?" The waitress came up to their table to check on them. She looked at Duevon lustfully as she licked her lips. He was used to women looking at him like he was water in the middle of the desert because he knew he was attractive.

Over 6ft and built from all of his working out on the field;

Duevon had hazel eyes, he wore his dreads in a nappy fade, and he had a perfect smile with deep dimples. Most women told him that he looked like the rapper 21 Savage. His rough around the edges demeanor made bitches want to jump his bones and see if he was as thuggish as he looked.

"Damn bitch, thirsty enough?" Stephanie asked the waitress angrily taking her attention from Duevon, while reminding her that there was a woman sitting across from him.

"My bad ma'am, I didn't mean any disrespect. I figured that this man was your son." The girl apologized to his mother.

"Damn,time for some more Botox injections that forty something age is shining through." He taunted Stephanie as he laughed at the girl's slick comment.

"Look little girl, do your job, and go ask the table over there do they want the flat or the seltzer water. I know the owner very well, and one word from me will have your ass over on Tulane at the unemployment office." Stephanie dismissed the waitress. The girl walked away quickly in embarrassment causing them both to laugh loudly at her.

"You are dead ass wrong mama, that girl was just doing her job. Now, if she hadn't come to check on us, you would have gone all Mama Dee on her. "As much money as we are spending why ain't nobody came to check on us?" He imitated his problematic mother while patting his head like a ghetto girl. He rolled his neck doing his worst drag queen impression.

Stephanie laughed at him loudly while clutching her stomach, "That wasn't checking on us, the little bitch was ready to snatch your dick out of your drawers and slide it down her throat. They act like they never saw a fine, rich man before. Then she tried to be cute with the ma'am shit like I look like an old lady. I'm sure I have the bitch by twenty years, but with the wide waist and those crooked teeth, she looks old enough to be my mama. Bad bitches only for my little man." She rolled her eyes and reached for her cell phone.

"You run the bad bitches away to. Face it, mama, no one will ever be good enough." Duevon retorted sadly as he felt a sharp pang in his heart. What had once been a funny joke had now taken a bad turn. Every time, he thought about his high school sweetheart and the fucked-up thing his mother did to her, his heart ached. It had been seven years, and every time it crossed his mind, he still had to find the nearest bottle of alcohol to numb the pain.

"Not this again. I did what I did to Kamya because I knew she wasn't good enough. You were both too young to be married. She would have held you back from your dreams. Stop bringing that shit up because I'm sick of hearing about it. Now, go ahead and pay the bill while I call the car to come to the front. I saw a bomb ass pair of Chanel boots that you are about to buy me because you love me so much." She retorted while standing from her seat and walking away from the table.

Duevon shook his head at her as he pulled his wallet out of the pocket of his Amiri's. He caught the waitress' eye from across the room who his mother had just cursed out and signaled for her to come back over to the table. Before she made it to the table fully, she was apologizing to him.

"I'm sooo sorry. I can't lose my job; I have two kids to take care of. I was out of line and even though you are extremely attractive, that was unprofessional of me," she rambled.

"My mother can be a bit extra sometimes. You are not losing your job; I actually called you over here to pay the check and give you a tip," he smiled at her warmly.

"So, you are fine, you look like money, and you're a sweetheart. Jesus pinch me because you can't be real." She blushed and walked away to close his tab.

"Don't start calling Jesus yet, I'm far from a saint," he murmured. He couldn't blame his mother for what happened to Kamya without three fingers pointing back at him. When the waitress returned, she placed the receipt in his hand, and he gave her his card. When she walked away to charge his credit card, he pulled out ten one-hundred-dollar bills and placed them underneath his plate.

Buy the babies a nice Halloween costume and plenty of candy. Don't take the credit either, tell them it's from player number 13 Duevon Howell.

He scribbled a note on a napkin and placed it next to the money. Halloween was a few weeks away and around this time all the prices of costumes, decorations, and candy had skyrocketed. If she was smart, she would dress their little asses in sheets, tell them they were ghosts, and take that money and pay up a few bills. If she was a single mother, working this low wage job, there was a fifty/fifty chance that at least one of her bills was past due. Duevon didn't look at life through rose-colored glasses, he had been through the struggle before, so he knew what it felt like. His father had walked out on him and his mother when he was an infant leaving her a struggling single mother trying to raise a black man. Stephanie had worked three jobs to maintain the household, pay for all the expensive ass football equipment he needed, all while still making it to every football practice and game whether it was at home or on the road. His mother had stepped for him every time. That was why he would do anything for her and give anything to her. He had finally made it to where they both worked so hard to get him to, so they both deserved to enjoy it. Somewhere along the way, she had forgotten about the struggle, but who was he to knock her off her high horse?

When the waitress returned from charging his card, she walked up to him and placed the card in his hands. "Thank you for your business," she told him nicely as she smiled at him.

"No problem," he smiled back and stood from the table. He walked away a few feet, before he heard a loud gasp from behind him. He chuckled slyly and turned his head back in her direction. She looked in his direction with tears filling her eyes and her hand over her mouth. He could tell that even though she worked among the wealthy she wasn't used to anyone doing something kind for her. It wasn't surprising. He had been rubbing elbows with the rich and famous for the past four years of his life, and he saw firsthand how selfish they could be. He knew that the waitress would never forget the act of kindness that he had bestowed upon her. Besides, he needed to put all the good karma he could into the universe to balance out all the hearts he had broken since he had lost the only girl he truly loved.

"Can't resist a charity case, can you?" His mother asked him when he slid inside of the backseat of their black-on-black Cadillac Escalade.

"Yeah, can't forget where you come from." He retorted while placing his dark Gucci glasses over his eyes and placing his head back to enjoy the ride.

Chapter Two

Nyasia Banks looked around her luxury condo on Common Street in awe. Coming from her shitty apartment in Atlanta, she could fit two of her old places inside of her new one and still have space leftover. The three-bedroom, two-bathroom unit had set her back a few hundred thousand but that was pennies compared to the money she had left over from her parent's hefty insurance policy. Thinking of her parent's, she began to grow sad all over again. It had been five months since they died in a car accident on the expressway 285, and every day it felt like it had just happened this morning. Despite all the money she had gotten in their settlement, all the money in the world couldn't buy happiness. Her parents had been the only family she had, and now she felt alone in the world. Everywhere she turned in Atlanta, she was reminded of them, so she decided to pick up and move last month to start fresh.

"Grief is healthy, and it has no expiration date. It is ok to be sad, it is ok to wish that my parents were still here." She told herself aloud as crippling anxiety began to consume her. She repeated her therapist's words over and over again and took long deep breaths until the anxiety passed. At twenty-one years' old, she was a college dropout, and the few friends that she had thought that she was crazy for picking up and moving away from the only city she had ever known. They told her that she would be lonely and New Orleans had barely survived a hurricane that could show up again at any moment. She didn't give a damn what they thought. New Orleans had always been a beautiful city to her. She loved the culture, the music, and the life that filled the city after all of the heartache and grief that Hurricane Katrina had caused. Her parent's death had taught her that tomorrow wasn't promised. She couldn't live her life full of what if's.

Bringing herself back to the present, she walked over to the kitchen of her new condo in search of something to whip up. When she opened the refrigerator, the only thing that was inside was what she had bought from the supermarket yesterday. Some bottles of water, a large fruit juice, and a few snacks were the only cuisine in sight. Rolling her eyes in aggravation, she went to her bedroom to grab a pair of shoes so she could run out to grab something to eat. She had finished unpacking last night and ordered from Uber Eats. Sick of fast food, she decided to head back to the market, and grab something to cook for the night.

When she stepped outside, she was greeted with a gentle breeze and all of the Halloween decorations for the upcoming holiday. When she was back home, her and her friends would get dressed in sexy costumes and hit up A Halloween party at the nearest club. This year, she would be in the house on Halloween night, binge watching scary movies, and scarfing down chocolate candy. That was fine with her, it was never too late to start new traditions.

Hitting the unlock button on her BMW jeep, she jumped inside and headed over to Central Grocery store. It was only a few miles up the road, and from what she had saw the last time she was there they had a large selection of fresh meat and vegetables. After walking around the store for forty-five minutes, she had picked up all the ingredients to make her favorite dish. Baked seafood scampi with jasmine rice and flat bread would be perfect for dinner. After paying for her purchases, she stepped back outside into the night. Even at nighttime, the city was full of lights and people bustling around, the city reminded her of a southern version of New York the city that never sleeps. She jumped into her car and started the engine. A few minutes later, her gas light popped on and a loud beeping sound filled the car's silence.

"SHIT." She said aloud as she looked at the gas mileage she had left. She didn't have enough gas to make it home, and she had no idea where the hell she was. Pulling out her cell phone, she looked up the nearest gas station and breathed a sigh of relief that it was two miles away. Turning on her GPS for directions, she hated stopping for gas in the middle of the night, but what other choice did she have?

When she finally pulled into the dimly lit gas station, there were no other cars there. Getting an eerie feeling, she dismissed her paranoia and placed her pepper spray inside of her purse. She pulled next to the pump and opened her driver side door to step out. She pulled out her card and looked around to make sure there was no one else around that could sneak up on her. The card reader slot looked a little worn, but she inserted her credit card inside anyway as she nervously tapped her foot.

PAYING AT PUMP PROHIBITED, SEE CASHIER

The warning message crossed the screen.

"Bullshit!" she stomped her feet hard. In these days where everyone used plastic, what type of rinky dink ass store would allow their card machine at the pump to be out of service. Slamming her door hard, she hit the lock button and walked up to the gas station. When she noticed that they had her favorite brand of wine, she grabbed a bottle and walked to the cashier's station.

"Can I get fifty on pump eight and this bottle of wine please?" she asked nicely while handing him her card.

"Quick second," he replied in a thick Arabian accent. She rolled her eyes as she looked around the store and out at her car while tapping her foot nervously. A few seconds later, a sexy guy walked into the store.

"I have things to do can you hurry this along?" she asked the clerk nervously.

"A little patience baby," the guy told her as he looked at her lustfully. Not bothering to answer him, she turned her attention back to the cashier and tapped on the window again. He finally accepted her payment and handed her a brown paper bag for her wine.

"You are sexy as hell, can I get to know you better?" The tall, built guy asked her in a New Orleans accent.

"No thank you, I don't talk to strangers." She retorted then flew past him quickly and went over to her car. Opening her driver door in case she needed a quick getaway; Nyasia pumped her gas impatiently.

When he came out of the store, she noticed that he had some sexy lips and dimples deep enough to hold water. A man with a beautiful smile was her weakness. Plus, he was headed her way.

"There ain't no reason to be rude baby," he persisted while walking up to a Mercedes jeep. She could tell by his swag, and his car that he had money, but so did she so she wasn't impressed. She could also tell that because he had money, he wasn't used to rejection.

"What part of no don't you understand the N or the O?" She snapped on him while finishing her gas transaction.

"Clearly you aren't from around here, but that stank ass attitude will get your ass touched in NOLA." He told her nastily causing the hairs on the back of her neck to stand up.

"Whatever. Not interested," she told him as she walked to the driver side door and jumped into the car quickly. Cranking the car, she sped away into the night before she got a chance to turn on her GPS. The only thing on her mind was getting away from the creepy guy as quickly as possible. She sped down the street and turned onto a side street, she then leaned over to her purse to grab her cell phone so she could get directions. When she finally had her phone in her hand, she began to type her address into the GPS, when suddenly her car began to move crazily from side to side.

"AAARGGHHHH!" she screamed loudly as she tried her best to control the wheel. Slamming down on the breaks, she came to a complete stop and put the car in park. She jumped out of the car quickly to see what the hell had happened and noticed that her driver side tire had gone completely flat.

"WHAT IN THE ENTIRE FUCK!" she screamed out as she kicked the tire hard and hurt her foot. Grabbing her toe, she hopped around on one foot as the pain shot up her leg. Tears filled her eyes as she tried her best to contain her emotions.

This was just great, she had caught a flat tire on the side of a dark ass road, and she had no idea where she was or how far from home she was. Getting back inside of the car, she turned on the lights, locked the door, and called for Triple A assistance. She had a spare tire in the back, but she had no idea how to put it on. Even if she did there was no way she was putting on a tire alone in the middle of the night.

After calling for help, she was disappointed to find that help wouldn't come for an hour, so she was literally stuck. Refusing to leave her car, she placed her head on the steering wheel in defeat and took deep breaths to calm herself. A few minutes later, a loud tap on her window startled her causing her to jump. When she looked at who was tapping on her window, she almost fainted. It was the sexy guy from the store.

"This man must have followed me. Oh my God maybe he flattened my tire while I was in the store. This nigga could be crazy, lord have mercy what the hell am I about to do?" Nyasia questioned as she reached into her purse and grabbed her pepper spray. She had never used it before, but tonight was going to be the night she was going to blind somebody's fine ass son.

"Whoa relax, I was about to help your crazy ass, but fuck it. Sit out here in the dark, and I hope you have more than that pepper spray because this is one of the most dangerous streets in the damn city," he told her angrily as he walked away from the car.

"NO WAIT!" she screamed out as she hit the automatic and rolled down the window. She peeked her head out and looked back at him.

"You have every right to be scared, but I'm not weird. I have a mother, and if she was in this situation, I would want somebody to help her. Even if she was a bitch to him," he told her. .

"Lord please protect me." Nyasia said a quick prayer to herself before placing the pepper spray on the passenger seat and stepping out of the car.

"I'm sorry. It's just like you said, I'm not from around these parts. You can't be too trusting out here especially as a woman," she laughed nervously and walked in the guy's direction. The closer she made it to him, the more she could smell his expensive cologne. He smelled so damn good; her mouth began to water.

"You must not know who I am?" he asked her while smirking.

"I have no idea," she retorted.

"Do you watch football? I play for the New Orleans Saints. My name is Duevon Howell jersey number thirteen. You can google me if it would make you feel safe. I don't prey on women, I have to fight bitches off this million-dollar dick," he told her cockily. He knew he wasn't the most popular player on the team, but he was still used to at least being recognized in his city. He was a rich nigga, and this girl was treating him like he was average.

"Well, it is nice to meet you Duevon. My name is Nyasia Banks, and I don't watch football and I'm not from here. I'm from Atlanta, and I just moved here at the end of November," she stuck her hand out to shake his. That was something else he wasn't used to. A woman had never treated him so formally and tried to shake his hand. Bitches always wanted to hug him so they could inhale his Bond number 9 cologne. This girl was definitely different, and she had his interest. Laughing it off, he reached out his hand and shook hers. His large hand swallowed her tiny hand and he found himself wanting to hold on a little longer. Not wanting to scare her because they were already in a dark alley, he took his hand back and placed it in his pocket.

"Do you have a spare? I can put it on for you in a few minutes and get you on about your way. Like I said earlier, this is not the safest spot for a woman to be when its dark," he reiterated.

Going to the car to grab her keys, she opened the trunk and directed him to her spare. She was so glad that even though she had been rude to him, he still stopped and helped her out. If the shoe had been on the other hand and someone had been rude to her, she would have laughed and rode right past their ass on the side of the road.

"Thank you again Duevon, you have to let me pay you. This is so incredibly nice of you." She told him as she shone her flashlight down to help him see the bolts as he loosened them.

"That's an insult I don't want your money," he dismissed her as he changed the tire.

Not wanting to stand in awkward silence, she engaged him in small talk. The conversation flowed smoothly, and he was done in no time. When he stood to his feet, he took the deflated tire to her trunk and placed it inside. He then closed it behind him and walked back up to her. She grabbed a bottle of hand sanitizer and placed a large amount in his hands so he could get the dirt off them.

"You have to let me give you something. I know I was rude earlier at the store, but I'm really not like that. I appreciate your help," Nyasia explained to him as she leaned up against her car. At first, she was falling over herself to get away from Duevon, but after giving him a chance she was beginning to like his personality. Granted, he was a little cocky and full of himself. However, being from Atlanta, Nyasia had met more than her fair share of athletes, rappers, producers, and people in the entertainment industry. They all held this same aura of cockiness, and it didn't faze her.

"Are you really, really appreciative?" Duevon asked her while stepping closer to her.

"I feel like I said that already. Can you just please let me repay you in some way," Nyasia laughed at his silliness.

"I can think of the perfect way." Duevon told her as he stepped a few inches closer. He towered over her forcing her to lean back to look up at his face. He was so close that she could smell the alcohol on his breath mixed with his cologne. Her face met his chest and she briefly imagined what it would be like to climb this large tree of a man that she was close enough to kiss. The moment was brief, and Nyasia quickly came to her senses.

"What are you getting at?" she stuttered as she looked up into his eyes. He leaned down and whispered in her ear, "Can I taste you Ms. Banks? If you really want to pay me back, let me take you to the Westin and eat your pussy until you lose count of how many times, I can make you cum. Afterwards I will fuck you better than any other nigga has ever fucked you before. Trust me I can back up all the shit I talk," he nibbled on her ear gently causing chills to go down her spine.

Snatching away from him, Nyasia reached out her hand and slapped Duevon harder than his mother ever had.

"WHY THE FUCK DID YOU DO THAT?" he asked her angrily as his face turned bright red.

"You just tried me like one of those little groupie hoes that hear your jersey number and go crazy. The appropriate thing would be for you to at least sit across the dinner table from me and make sure I have proper hygiene before you offer to bury your face in my pussy. I KNOW YOU MAY NOT HEAR THIS OFTEN, but there ain't shit you can do for me that I can't do for myself. Go try the next woman like trash, you may get further," Nyasia spat disrespectfully as she walked back to her car and got inside while slamming the door. She had tried her hardest not to judge Duevon, but he had turned out to be exactly the type of nigga she thought he was when she laid eyes on him in the gas station. His looks made him entitled as hell and the money and status only hurt the situation worse. He needed a large slice of humble pie, and he had met the right bitch to deliver it to him.

She sat in her driver seat and reached for her wallet in her purse, she then pulled out three one-hundred-dollar bills, backed up to where he was still standing with his mouth wide open, and tossed the money in his face. She then sped off down the street this time being careful to make sure she wasn't rolling over anything that could flatten another tire.

Duevon laughed loudly at the exchange and as she pulled away, he looked down at her license plate. Using his photographic memory, he remembered her plate number as she pulled away.

Ms. Banks had him even more intrigued than she did at first. He had used that same line on several women and their panties had dropped so fast, he didn't even have time to catch them. The fact that she was different only made him even more determined to get her. There was nothing that he couldn't have, and she would be no exception. He would make her eat those same words, with her face in his pillows and her ass tooted up in the air.

"Who is it?" Nyasia loudly asked two days later as someone beat on her door like the police.

"Delivery," the man repeated slowly like she was hard of hearing. Looking out of the peephole, she saw that he held a box in his hand, and he was dressed professionally. Shrugging, she opened the door. "I didn't order anything are you sure you have the right address?" she questioned him as she stood there with a crop top and a pair of black leggings.

She had been curled up on her couch with a comfy throw blanket reading a book called, *All Snakes Don't Hiss* by her favorite author O'sharra. The book was recommended to her in a book group on Facebook, and just as the other readers had said she couldn't put it down. Since she was a child Nyasia had loved to read. It was one of the things her and her mother had in common. They would often recommend books to each other all the time, then talk about them over lunch when her mother could get away from the office. As the best real estate agent in Atlanta, her mother was always booked and busy so Nyasia cherished the moments when they could have lunch and bond over bomb ass urban fiction books.

"The order is for a Ms. Nyasia Banks is that you?" the driver asked in his thick accent.

"Yes, that's me. You are at the right address, so I won't make your job any harder" Nyasia replied grabbing for the box and signing her name on the electronic keypad. She was half curious to see what the hell was in the box and half ready to just get back to her damn book. Standing in the doorway going back and forth with the delivery guy wasn't going to make the exchange go any quicker.

After signing for the box, she kicked the door closed behind herself and walked over to the dining room table. Thanks to an interior designer she had found on Instagram and the best furniture store in New Orleans, her place was now fully decorated and furnished. Putting the box on the table, she used her sharp stiletto nail to slice the tape and opened the box. Inside was a porcelain bowl filled with the prettiest roses she had ever laid eyes on, and an elegant note sitting on top.

I was wrong with the way I came at you the other night. Please accept my apology. It's hard to teach an old dog new tricks, but I'm willing to learn how to treat a lady like she deserves to be treated, I just need a little direction. I would love for you to call me and accept an invitation to dinner. My number is 504-232-1254.

P.S these will keep coming every day in every color until you agree to have dinner with me. Just one dinner! Everyone has to eat - Duevon

Nyasia smiled broadly at the beautiful flower arrangement and the sweet note. She had been thinking about Duevon since their strange encounter and even though he was nasty as hell, his little offer had definitely made her pussy thump. She hadn't been fucked by anyone except her vibrator since her parent's had died and she was fiending for a good orgasm. She had run her batteries out of her vibrator thinking about Duevon and pretending that it was him inside of her instead of the mechanical toy. Nyasia was far from a virgin, but she had too much self-respect to just be out fucking different men and partaking in all this sneaky link culture. Her parents had raised her better than that, and they would turn in their grave from disappointment if she just threw all of their teachings out the window. It was bad enough she had dropped out of college; she couldn't disappoint them even further by just being some boy's jump off.

Deciding to make him sweat a little, Nyasia put the vase up in her apartment and ripped up his note. She had to let him know that he was fucking with a real one. Men complained about difficult women, but deep down the chase made their dick harder than a College Calculus test. Sitting back down in her comfortable spot, Nyasia opened her book and finished reading about the drama.

Chapter Three

"WHERE THE HELL IS YOUR HEAD HOWELL?" Coach Allen called out angrily. They were doing drills to prepare for their game against the Patriots tomorrow and Duevon's mind was somewhere else. His footwork was sloppy, he hadn't been catching any of the passes, and all of the defensive players were slipping by him easily.

"One more wrong play and your ass is riding the bench. I won't let you embarrass me on the field tomorrow!" the couch told him angrily as he brought him a Gatorade and a white towel to wipe his face. Removing his helmet, he reached for the drink and took a long sip. It was the beginning of October, around this time every year, he began to go into a deep depression. Even though he had tried to forget about the worst night of his life, being this close to Halloween reminded him of Kamya's death. She hadn't deserved what him and his mother had done to her, but he was caught between a rock and a hard place. How was he supposed to choose between the woman that had given him life and the girl he loved with all his heart?

"My bad coach, I had a long night. I just need some rest and a good massage. I swear I will have it together tomorrow." Duevon pleaded as he walked behind his coach and off the field. Football was his life, and he loved the sport more than his next breath. Every game he sat out was forty thousand dollars against his pay, and he couldn't afford to miss that kind of money.

"I told you when you signed on to this team, that the money, alcohol, and women could easily be your downfall. It's not enough to just have talent, you have to have discipline as well," coach

Allen scolded him. "I won't bench you, but I expect for you to get out on this field tomorrow and show me the hungry young man I recruited. Take your ass home, get some rest, no alcohol tonight and leave the groupies alone. You need to have all your strength for tomorrow," Coach dismissed him. Thankful that he wasn't getting benched, Duevon nodded his head sadly, and walked to the locker room so that he could shower and get out of his uniform. Every part of him wanted to have a drink and drown his sorrows, but he refused to disobey his coach's direct orders.

After a hot shower and slipping on sweats, a t-shirt, and some Nike dunks; he reached for his phone and went over to his notifications. He had a missed call from his mother, and one text message. Going over to his messages, he smiled when he saw the 404-area code. That was an Atlanta number, and he only knew one hottie from Atlanta. It had taken her long enough, but she had finally decided to use a nigga's number.

If you send one more set of roses to my house, it's going to look like a flower shop or a funeral home. I'm free for dinner tonight if you are

The text from Nyasia read. Just like he had told her in his written note, he was going to send flowers to her house every day until she agreed to go out with him. It had been a week since he met her, and he had kept his word of sending her a bouquet of roses, of a different color, every day. He was prepared to send her roses for a month if that was what it took to see her again. Money wasn't a thing to him, and Ms. Nyasia Banks had plagued his thoughts since the day she threw multiple one-hundred-dollar bills in his face like he was a stripper at Magic City. Instead of pissing him off, it had turned him on.

"It took you long enough." Duevon texted her back cockily as he smiled and bit his bottom lip. He was one step closer to getting between her thick thighs and the anticipation made his mouth water.

"How about I make your smart ass wait another week,

goodbye." She texted him back less than a second after he had sent his smart reply back to her. He loved verbal sparring; it was definitely a form of foreplay in his book. A woman that talked shit and didn't bow down to him only made him want to go harder, to make her stand on all the shit she said.

I can't wait another week baby. I'm fiending for some Ms. Banks. I will behave I promise. Does tonight at 9pm work for you? I can either come and pick you up, or you can meet me at Kirklands. They have the best wine selection and seafood gumbo in Nawlins

He texted her back and waited anxiously for her to reply. When the three dots popped up signaling that she was in the middle of her message, he watched the screen patiently. Suddenly the dots disappeared, a few seconds later they reappeared. He laughed out loud like a high school boy with his first crush. Clearly Nyasia hadn't expected him to concede so easily. From their few encounters, Duevon could tell that she was an independent woman that liked control. The best way to deal with those types, were to make them feel as if they were in control. Sure, she could win the battle, but Duevon planned to win the war.

"It's a little soon for me to ride in the car with you. I will meet you there 9pm sharp and don't be late! Don't make me regret telling you yes," she texted back.

He smiled and grabbed his duffel from his locker, placing all of his things in it. Just like that his shitty mood had been lifted. He couldn't wait to get home, change into something fly, and sit across from Nyasia at the dinner table. As if she could sense he was happy, his mother called him again.

"Yes mother," he answered the phone in annoyance.

"That is no way to answer the phone for your mother nigga have some respect!" His mother yelled at him causing him to bite his lip to keep the words he wanted to tell her in his mouth. She had a way of talking to him like he was a little child and he wanted to correct her, but he didn't want to make her angry. Stephanie was a different type of beast when she was angry.

"Yes, my beautiful mother, how are you this evening?" Duevon asked her with sarcasm.

"Don't be funny, big head ass boy. I just ended my call with your coach and I'm not liking what I'm hearing. He says that you seem as if your head is not in the game. I sent Stedman to come and get you. A friend of his agreed to ride with him so that he could drive your car home. I want you to come straight here. I'm going to cook all of your favorites, and we will watch a few home movies of your game highlights. Some of the best players lose their heads, but we are going to get through this. You are going to whip Russel Wilson's ass so bad on that field tomorrow, his wife is going to want to give you her goodies," Stephanie laughed at her own terrible joke.

Normally Duevon would have done exactly as his mother instructed. It was too big of a hassle to challenge her, so he had learned to just go with the flow when she made plans. However, tonight was different. He had made plans with a gorgeous woman that he couldn't get off his mind. He wasn't about to go home with a hard dick and watch home movies with his mother. He also knew that he couldn't come straight out and tell his mother, that he wasn't about to come home and watch movies with her. He had to think of a smooth way to get out of this shit without making her suspicious. If she knew that he was blowing her off to be with a bitch she would paint New Orleans red looking for his ass. She would then bust up in the restaurant and act a fool. She had done it before, but he wouldn't let her do it this time. Nyasia wasn't one of those groupie girls that would let his mama disrespect her and still be on his dick. Hell, she wouldn't even let him come at her crazy.

Laughing at her joke with her to play it off, Duevon cleared his throat before he began to lie. "You are silly as hell. I was just about t call you and tell you that I was already going to go over some plays with a few teammates tonight. Tomorrow is a really big game for us, so we have to be on one accord with each other." He lied easily as he walked out of the building looking around for his overpaid security guard/babysitter.

"You don't need to be on an accord with them, you need to get your own head in the game. This is not the time to worry about anyone else," Stephanie protested.

"But you are the one that's always preaching that there is no I in team. You are always the one trying to get me to connect more with the other players. Is that right or wrong?" He threw her words up in her face as he walked up to his car door and placed the key in the door to unlock it. He didn't want to unlock the car from his key fob, because it would make a loud chirp noise and he didn't want his mother to know that he had already made it outside to his car.

"Well yeah… I… I did say that." His mother stuttered as she fumbled through her words.

"This is the first time I have been invited over any of the player's house. They are finally starting to see me as part of the team and not just some kid, because I'm the youngest. They are finally starting to see my potential," he lied.

"Yes, I was a little sloppy on the field today, but they offered to help me turn it around for the game tomorrow," he laid it on thick causing his mother to be speechless. He drove through the streets of New Orleans towards the bank. He had three hours to meet Nyasia and he could no longer change clothes at home like he originally planned. His mother could tell when he was lying just by looking at him. Instead, he planned to grab some cash, go over to his favorite male boutique in town, pick out some fly shit, and get dressed right there in the store. He knew the owner personally, so it wouldn't be a problem. He also planned to pull off enough cash to pay for dinner, and a nice hotel suite if he were to get lucky. He wouldn't make the same mistake of charging the clothes, restaurant, and room to his card. His nosey ass mother would see his whereabouts based on the transactions and best-case scenario question him about how he could be shopping when he claimed to be at his teammates house. Worst case scenario, she would show up at the last place he swiped the card looking for him like a damn private investigator.

"I guess you are right," she agreed.

"I still think you should let the driver take you though. You may want to have some drinks with the guys, and I hate when you drink and drive," his mother lied. The real reason she wanted the driver to take him was so that she could verify his whereabouts like she was a probation officer. There was no future in flexing, they both knew it.

"That would have been a great idea mom, but I'm halfway here already," he lied to her as he turned on the street of the Chase bank. "The whole time we were talking, I was already enroute. I was so excited to be getting an invite that I headed straight here," he lied.

"As a matter of fact, I'm riding past a police car, and you know it's against the law to ride and talk on the phone. Let me call you right back when I'm not around him anymore," Duevon ended the call. He had pulled in front of the bank and parked his car. He walked up to the bank, made a cash withdrawal, then got back in the car and sped away like he had just robbed the atm. It was a shame that he had to steal money from his own account to take out a woman. Money that he had worked hard and sweated for. This shit with his mother was pushing him over the edge, and he was caught between a rock and a hard place. His love for her and his independence were playing tug of war, and he was the rag doll in the middle, with his arms outstretched getting pulled to both sides. "Eventually she will let up. I just have to give her a little more time," he told himself. The problem was he knew that he was lying. He had been saying the same lie to himself since he was a teenager.

As if she had alerts telling her when his card was swiped, his phone began to ring.

"Like fucking clockwork," Duevon looked up to the roof if his car in aggravation. He then looked down at the screen of his phone wanting it to be someone else, but already knowing who was calling. It was his mother. Again.

"DUEVON WHAT THE FUCK IS GOING ON? I just got an alert that three thousand dollars was withdrawn from your account. Did you pull that money out? Did someone steal your card? Go to your bank app and lock your card right now! First thing in the morning, I will call down to the bank and speak with their fraud department. Nobody is going to take shit from us and think it's just sweet," his mother ranted angrily. He didn't understand how someone was taking anything from them when every cent of the money belonged to him.

"Ma calm down. No one took anything from me," he put an emphasis on me to remind her that there was no them. "I took my own money. I wanted to grab a few things for the get together. I know I told you I wasn't drinking, but I can't guarantee that they won't be drinking. I'm going to buy a few bottles to contribute. These are athletes. They are rich niggas, and I can't sit around them and look broke. That's not a problem, is it? With me taking my own money from my bank," he snapped on her.

"I was just trying to make sure your little ass hadn't been robbed. I'm looking out for you, and this is the stank ass reply you want to give me?" his mother began screaming loudly like a hyena. He shook his head because he already knew where she was going with this. She was extremely toxic, and this was the part of the conversation when she would try to manipulate him into feeling like he was wrong for standing up for himself. He refused to feed into her negative ass energy, then carry that same negativity around for the rest of the evening. "It's cool I know you didn't mean any harm. Everything is taken care of though," he retorted smoothly not allowing her to get him out of character. "Let me call you back this is my team mate on the other line, I know they are trying to figure out why I still haven't made it yet," he told her.

"Right even though you were halfway there the last time we talked," she hung up in his face rudely. She was on to his ass, and she knew that he was lying. However, she didn't know where he was, so there wasn't shit she could do about it but have an attitude. That was why she was really mad.

After going to Fly Guy's Boutique and dropping a bag, on a pair of men spiked Christian Louboutin's, a pair of Aimri jeans, and the matching button-down shirt; Duevon stepped into the fitting room and changed out of his casual clothes. Butterflies filled his stomach for the first time in a while and he realized that he was feeling excited. When he stepped out of the room, he admired himself from head to toe. He looked damn good, and there was no way Nyasia would be able to deny him.

"You are looking fresh bro. Now you need the fragrance to set that shit off," the owner told him as he walked over to him with a tray of scents for men.

"I have Creed, Versace, Bond no 9, Gucci. Which one are you going with?" he asked Duevon "Give me the Creed. The last time she saw me I had on the Bond. So, I have to switch up on her," Duevon smiled. He then went through his wallet and handed the owner eleven one-hundred-dollar bills.

"Thank you for supporting black business's brother," the owner hit hands with him in a one-sided embrace.

"Always," Duevon retorted while posing for a quick selfie with the owner for his Instagram page.

"Do me a favor and post it tomorrow. Groupies be on a nigga body and niggas be hating, not trying to get Pop Smoked out here," Duevon told the owner. It was partly the truth. Half of him didn't want Stephanie seeing him at Fly Guy's and being in his business the other half of him knew that as a professional athlete he had to move smart. There had been an increasing number of robberies and murders against people in the entertainment industry. People didn't understand that even though he played side by side with Drew Brees he wasn't touching half of the money that the superstar QB was seeing. Athletes could wear the same uniform, play at the same time, be on the same team, and make different salaries.

Duevon wasn't the richest player on the team, but with all of the flashy purchases he made, the average person would definitely think he had M's in his bank account. That was why he had chosen Kirkland's as a place to meet Nyasia. Not only was the restaurant upscale, but it was also in the nice area of New Orleans. Only people of a certain tax bracket visited this place. The authorities made sure that a fly wouldn't land anywhere near their overpriced heads. That would be good for both his safety and his image. He had done his research on Nyasia. The condo she owned cost more than most people made in a year, and her whip was foreign. Not to mention she throwed money at him like he was the broke one. Her aura screamed that either she had a rich ass sugar daddy, or she came from money.

"Yeah, you can't be too careful out here. I got you, and I won't post this until tomorrow. Be safe but stay dangerous," the owner retorted as he shook hands with Duevon again and let him out of the store. He could tell that the owner was a reformed street nigga that had probably taken his illegal funds and invested them into a profitable business. Dismissing thoughts of things that had nothing to do with him, Duevon floated to his car on cloud nine. The chilly night air didn't even bother him like it usually did. When a person was truly happy, they didn't sweat small shit He looked down at the AP on his wrist to see how much time he had left. It would be nine in an hour and the restaurant was still thirty minutes away. Deciding that he would rather be early and wait for her, Duevon drove in the direction of Kirkland's blasting Da Baby's latest mixtape.

When he finally made it to the restaurant, he was greeted by the waitress and led over to the table. He looked down at his wrist and it was fifteen minutes until. Deciding to order a drink while he waited, ten minutes later he was floored when he laid eyes on his date. Nyasia wore a sexy red dress and turned heads as she walked towards their table. The dress hugged her curves, but it didn't look cheap. She looked effortlessly sexy, and her long hair was pinned into a sleek updo. Standing from the table, Duevon smiled at his gorgeous date.

"Early huh?" he questioned as he slid her chair from the table respectfully.

"You know what that say, when you are on time you are late. I appreciate you for being early I thought that I was going to beat you here," she blushed as she sat in the seat.

"It's ok, you have been judging me since you met me." He retorted playfully causing her to laugh.

"Can you blame me? You came at me wrong from the beginning.," she quipped.

"Yes, that was tasteless of me, and I apologize. I'm so used to everything I say or do being a turn on to women, that I felt like you would go for it. You showed me you were different and, I respect you for that. I would be lying if I said I wasn't fantasizing about taking you in the bathroom and sliding that dress up over your hips," he began as he licked his lips at her seductively.

"I'm gone," she told him while pushing away from the table before he could catch her hand.

"I'm playing," he laughed.

"I promised you I would behave, and I'm going to keep that promise." He held her hand as she looked at him sideways.

When the waitress arrived, he ordered for them both and Nyasia was impressed. They began to get into a deep conversation as they got to know each other better. Minutes turned into hours, as they feasted, laughed, and shared stories from their childhood. They were the last ones in the restaurant, and they didn't even notice that it was past closing time. When the waitress came to their table for the last time, she politely brought them their check and stood waiting. Catching the hint that it was time to go, they laughed as they walked out of the door.

"I had an amazing time with you Duevon," Nyasia told him as he walked her to her car.

"I had a, even better time with you," Duevon leaned against her car. "I'm honestly not ready for the night to end," he told her bashfully. The smile from her face faded and turned into a grimace.

"Don't start Duevon we had a really nice date, but if you think I'm going to go home with you just because you spent a few dollars on a meal," she began before he cut her off.

"I was just going to say that I know this beautiful bayou that we could take a walk near and talk a bit more. I'm not trying to get in your pants Nyasia. You make me laugh, and a nigga had a pretty rough day at practice. I have a big game tomorrow and I'm sort of stressed. I could just use a little more of your company if you feel up to it," he told her honestly. Even though he had come into the restaurant with the intentions of smooth talking and taking her back to his room, she had been such a vibe that he hadn't thought about fucking again for the remainder of the dinner. She had made him laugh, completely taken his mind off the shit he was going through with his mother, and his shortcomings at practice today. Her energy was magnetic, and he loved being in her presence.

Searching his eyes to see if she could see truth in his statement, she noticed that he seemed genuine. He had been a gentleman the entire evening, and she was in no rush to get back to her lavish but lonely apartment. Nodding her head, she placed her keys in her purse, and slipped her hand into his. He smiled at her, and they began to walk and enjoy more of each other's company.

Chapter Four

"What do you mean he gave you the night off? You don't work for him you work for me motherfucker. As a matter of fact, you worked for me. As in past tense. Your ass is fired," Stephanie told Stedman angrily as she ended the call in his face.Duevon had been spending less time at home and more time out God knows where. Stedman's useless ass never had a report for her about her son's whereabouts, so she was no longer in need of his services. She couldn't lie, Duevon had been playing his ass off on the field. He also had been happier lately than she had seen him in a long time. Stephanie knew Duevon better than he knew himself, and the only thing that could make her son glow like a kid on Christmas was a bitch. There was definitely someone new in his life, but no matter how hard she tried she couldn't catch him in the act.

Tonight, was his big game against the Cardinals, and she had lied and told him that she had a terrible headache so she couldn't make it. He didn't sound torn up about it as he told her to feel better and rushed her off the phone. She knew that if he was dating someone seriously, the little hussy would be at his game if he thought that she wasn't coming. It was time for her to find out about the whore that had her little boy's nose wide open. He was just a kid and he needed her to protect him from these money hungry witches. Besides, their favorite holiday Halloween was a week away. Unbeknownst to him she was throwing a huge costume party, and she wanted to personally invite his coach and his teammates. If she left it up to him to invite them, he would probably forget like he always did. He may have thought that he was grown, but he needed his mother, and he would always need her. Duevon had left home earlier so that he could get a last-minute practice in, and Stephanie looked through her closet to find something fly to wear to the game. Deciding on a pair of jeans that looked painted on, a sexy off the shoulder sweater, and a pair of thigh-high Fendi boots, she took her time and got dressed being sure that not one single hair was out of place.

When Stephanie made it to the arena, she walked up to the VIP entrance and showed the security guards her ticket. She had a season pass, and the best seats in the house. She sat amongst the celebrities, and the wives and girlfriends of the other players as the waiters catered to her every need.

"Hey Teyana girl I didn't know you were in town," she greeted the model, wife of famous basketball player Iman, and social media influencer.

"Hey Stephanie, how is everything? Your son has been stepping on necks all season. I was down in Vegas last week and I bet on him, made a quick 30 bands," Teyana praised Duevon causing Stephanie to blush.

"That's my boy," she smiled and waved her hand dismissively as she hugged the star and made her way over to her seat. As she looked around, she spoke to a few other high-profile celebrities. She could name every person in the room, until her eyes focused on one young woman that she had never seen before. Dressed too fly to be a groupie, the first thing that Stephanie noticed about her was her beauty. Her caramel complexion glowed, her body was tight, and the three-thousand-dollar Balenciaga boots she wore had been on the runway only last month. She sipped from a flute of champagne like she belonged there as she watched the game intensely. A gut feeling told Stephanie to keep an eye on this bitch.

After a successful game, the skybox was lit as champagne, oysters and caviar flowed. Stephanie had noticed that the young girl had kept to herself the entire game. She was definitely here for one of the players. When the team walked through the door, after getting cleaned up, cheers floated through the room as they were congratulated by everyone. When Duevon walked into the room, he wore the biggest smile she had ever seen. She was so proud of her handsome boy, and she stood from her seat to get up and hug him. Before she could stand fully, Duevon walked past her and ran up to the young lady that Stephanie had been eyeing all night. Her stomach balled up as he grabbed her from the seat and twirled her in the air like a princess. He then placed the biggest, juiciest kiss on her full lips as if they were the only two people in the room. She laughed as he held her tight. Catching her second wind, Stephanie stood from her seat and walked over to Duevon angrily.

"Good game son!" He spat disrespectfully causing Duevon to jump as if he had been caught doing something he had no business doing.

"Heyy mama," Duevon stuttered as he avoided eye contact with Stephanie and placed Nyasia back on her feet. The moment had gone from perfect to awkward in less than a minute.

"I thought you weren't feeling too good, so you couldn't come out tonight." He told her while continuing to avoid her eyes.

"Nothing a little Tylenol couldn't fix. I would never miss my little boy's game are you crazy?" she asked him while flashing an evil smile at the girl who stood looking at her unfazed.

"Introduce me to your little friend," she looked at the girl up and down like she was a piece of trash. The young woman looked taken aback by her blunt words, but she didn't give a fuck. It was time this bitch found out who was in charge around here. Her son had probably bought everything the little wench had on. She was noticing more and more that Duevon was pulling cash from his account, but she didn't see him with any shopping bags, any new jewelry, and he hadn't bought a new car. She would bet the twenty-thousand-dollar chain on her neck, that her son had been spending his money on this little thot and that shit stopped today.

"My name is Nyasia ma'am and there's nothing little about me." Nyasia snapped back on her before giving Duevon a chance to speak.

"Babe, she didn't mean it that way. She only meant that you are younger than me. You know you have a baby face" Duevon tried to interject before Stephanie cut him off.

"You are a little friend if I say you are bitch. Just because you might be sucking his dick good enough for him to put you in designer shoes, that doesn't mean that you actually mean something." Stephanie laughed as she placed her glass of champagne to her mouth and took a long sip while never breaking eye contact with the young girl.

"Now mom you know that was inappropriate." Duevon defended Nyasia as she mugged his mother hatefully. He had tried to defend her first fucked up comment even though all three of them knew she was belittling Nyasia. Now she was following up the bad statement with an even worse comment.

"Your son hasn't spent one cent on me lady, from the looks of it he is spending all his money on you. That fake ass body, and Botox can't hide the fact that your neck is saggy bitch. Might be time for your baby boy to pay for a face lift old bird," she retorted as Stephanie lunged at her.

"OH SHIT CALL SECURITY!" someone screamed out.

"I'm going to show you a, old bird bitch, I'm about to whip your young ass," she tried desperately to get around Duevon as he stood between the two of them shielding Nyasia.

"You better get your mother before I knock those big ass chiclets out of her mouth. Did the doctor even bother to measure those big ass teeth before he shoved them in your mouth? You are out here looking like Denzel and Donatella Versace had a baby. Don't walk past a fire because all that plastic looks flammable." Nyasia spat causing Duevon to chuckle slightly. Angry that he had the laughed at the little disrespectful bitch's comments, Stephanie slapped him hard across the face.

"What the fuck are you laughing at?" she yelled as security

approached.

"Mr. Howell, are you ok? Would you like for us to remove this woman?" two big bouncers looked at Stephanie like she was a nobody.

"Y'all came just in time to remove this little thot. I'm his mother. I am supposed to be here!" Stephanie yelled out as all eyes were on the spectacle they were creating.

"They don't have to remove shit because I'm out of here. You think because he is your son you can talk to me crazy, and I'm not going to get back with your ass? Unlike them, I don't have to bow down to you for your son to throw me crumbs. Wrong bitch," Nyasia retorted as she grabbed her Birkin bag and attempted to walk away. Duevon grabbed her arm and stopped her from leaving.

"Actually, you can remove my mother. I think she has had a few too many glasses of champagne and she might need to sleep it off," he told them angrily as he looked at Stephanie. Her handprint was etched into his face because he was so brown skinned, and she had slapped him with so much force.

"Are you fucking serious?" she looked at her son as if he had lost his mind.

"Time to go ma'am," the security grabbed her and escorted her to the exit. She was mortified as all of the celebrities she had just been talking to looked at her like she was an angry fan that had gotten out of control. Even Teyana looked down her nose at Stephanie like she smelled like garbage.

"Don't touch me I can walk by my damn self," Stephanie snatched away from the security as she walked out of the door with her head held high. She couldn't believe that her only son had chosen this bitch over her. After all she had done to get him to where he was. After all of the sacrifices she had made for him. He had the nerve to let a bitch he had just started fucking with corrupt his mind against her.

"What the hell was that about?" Nyasia asked him angrily when his mother walked out of the door. She was embarrassed as hell. She had never in her life disrespected someone that was old enough to be her mother and she felt sick to her stomach.

Grabbing her hand, Duevon led her out of the alternative exit into the hallway.

"My mother can be a little overprotective that's all. That has nothing to do with us. I'm sorry she came at you that way. It won't happen again," Duevon tried to convince her as she shook her head.

"Maybe we shouldn't be friends Duevon, I mean I'm not accustomed to anyone's mother coming at me that way, and I would never ask you to choose me over the woman that brought you in this world," she told him as she looked away.

"She didn't bring me in this world, I was adopted. Yes, she has taken care of me, and I would never choose anyone over her, but right is right and wrong is wrong. You have to give respect to get it I don't give a fuck if you are eight or eighty. She has become too comfortable with cursing out women that I mess with. I am ashamed to say, she has even put her hands on a few of them. These past few weeks that we have been dating have meant a lot to me and if you no longer want to see me then I would rather it be because of something I did wrong. Don't let my mother run you away. I apologize for the way she acted," he told Nyasia sincerely as he rubbed the side of her face. The only reason he had invited her out tonight was because Stephanie had told him that she wouldn't be here. She had tricked him, made him look like a little boy in front of his teammates, his celebrity friends, and Nyasia. She deserved to be escorted out of the room for coming at someone crazy who she didn't even know. Duevon didn't feel any remorse for her.

"I have enjoyed our time together as well Duevon, and I don't want us to stop being friends. Even though she came at me wrong, I was raised better than how I acted, and I apologize to you for saying those things to your mother," she looked away from him. Out of all the bitches that Stephanie had cursed out and fought, none of them ever had any remorse about cursing her back out. Nyasia had been raised with respect and he liked that about her.

Reaching for her chin to pull her face up, he leaned down to kiss her. This was their first kiss and even though he had tried to refrain from showing her any physical affection while they had been dating for the past few weeks, the moment felt right so he went for it.

At first, she was reluctant to kiss him back. Duevon thought that maybe he had misread the signs, until her full lips parted, and she began to kiss him back feverishly. Nyasia allowed herself to be swept up in the moment, as Duevon kissed her. She had wanted him just as bad as he wanted her. However, she didn't know if he really liked her or if he just enjoyed the thrill of chasing her. He had told her over and over again that she wasn't making things easy for him like he was used to. A part of her was worried that he just wanted to check her off his to do list. For the past few weeks, they had been hanging out every day. They went on dates, he showed her around his city, and they enjoyed each other's company. Being careful not to give the wrong impression, she never invited him inside of her condo, and never tried to go to his house or any other intimate places. She Could be strong in public, but she knew behind closed doors, Duevon could easily make her weak, so she didn't put herself in the position to be alone with him. One lingering look from him and her ass would fold like laundry.

When the kiss ended, they stood looking at each other intensely. Neither one of them had the words to say in that moment, so silence spoke for them. When Duevon reached for her hand, she placed her hand in his and let him lead her outside of the arena. Unbeknownst to them, Stephanie had paid the guards a thousand dollars a piece to let her go. From the shadows, she watched and heard the whole encounter between Duevon and Nyasia. She had never told Duevon that he was adopted, so she didn't know how the hell he knew. When he was younger, he sometimes questioned her about why they didn't look alike. She would always tell him that he looked like his father that had walked out on them when he was a baby. Eventually the questions stopped, and she thought that he had accepted her answers as truth. Tears filled her eyes as his betrayal set in. He had known that he was adopted, but never told her that he knew. He had trusted this bitch that he had only been dating for a few weeks with some information this important, and that burned Stephanie's soul.

She hated what she was about to do next, but she had the perfect idea to kill two birds with one stone. She would pay her son back for the bullshit he had just pulled, and she would get this bitch out of his life simultaneously. It would hurt her more than it hurt him to have to punish him, but like the bible said children were meant to be disciplined by their parents when they did wrong. It was time to spank the baby for going up against the bitch that had created him from nothing.Had it not been for her he would have ended up a nobody with NFL dreams like a million other little boys around the world. She had been his manager, marketer, put him in the right places at the right times and this was how he repaid her.

"Good Luck," Justin's words rang out in her head as she followed the two lovebirds out of the arena. She made sure not to follow too closely, to alert them that she was near. She watched him interact with Nyasia like she was the Queen of Fucking England. Nyasia had told Stephanie that she had the "wrong bitch" but in actuality, it was her who had the wrong bitch. Stephanie wasn't the type of woman that would walk away from a fight easily.

It had begun to rain outside of the arena and people ran quickly to avoid getting wet. Stephanie didn't run, she walked. A bad bitch didn't fear water or getting her hair wet. Her expensive wig, clothes, and shoes could all easily be replaced as long as she kept her cash cow underneath her arm. The minute another bitch got Into Duevon's head, Stephanie feared that her funds and lifestyle would stop. Once you got accustomed to steak there was no way you would settle for less than.

"We are all we have, and all we need." Stephanie said aloud as she watched Duevon open the door for Nyasia and make sure she was safely tucked inside before he ran around to get into the driver side of the car. Stephanie stood in the rain and watched the car drive away as her soaking wet hair clung to her face and her clothes clung to her body. Her flawless makeup was now ruined, and it ran down her face like a clown, as her tears mixed with rain.

Chapter Five

As word about Duevon and Nyasia dating spread throughout the city, the number of bitches that threw themselves at Duevon began to multiply. He had been getting his fair share of pussy before he began seriously dating Nyasia, but it was as being with her had magnified his worth in the eyes of other women. Women were so bold that he and Nyasia could be on a date and a waitress would blatantly flirt with him in her face. She had finally gotten him to do what no other groupie in New Orleans could get him to do, date and take a woman seriously. In their minds, if he was capable of exclusively dating, he was capable of being in a relationship. If he could be in a relationship, he could propose and be a husband. Single women knew that it was easier to get a nigga in a relationship or a nigga that was married to leave his woman, than it was to get a single man to be serious about one woman.

All of the attention didn't bother Nyasia. She knew her worth, and she knew what she brought to the table. Seeing women fawn over Devon didn't pressure her to sleep with him and made her only more determined to make him wait for the pussy. Unlike them she didn't want or need him for a thing. The way she reciprocated his energy only made him crazier about her. She had no problem paying for dates, and spoiling him back, unlike the women from his past who always had their hands out for him to put something in them. The only suspicious thing about Nyasia was in all of the time that they had been dating, he still had no idea how she had so much money. He didn't see her going to work. The fact that they had talked about so much, but she kept so many things private had begun to eat at him. One day over dinner, he decided to just come out and ask her. He had shared things with her that he had never told a soul, not even his first love. After weeks of dating he felt that he deserved to know what she did for a living.

They had just finished dinner at a lavish restaurant, and when the waitress brought the bill, his eyes bulged at the price. The total had come up to five hundred and fifty-seven dollars. Reaching for his wallet to pay, Nyasia watched how the waitress lustfully watched him. Just to be petty, she plucked the bill from his hand. She then reached into her oversized Louis Vuitton monogram bag, pulled out her matching wallet, and took her black card from it. Putting the card on the bill, she smirked as the bitch. Duevon smiled at her then back at the waitress as if to say, "Could you afford to do the same?" The waitress looked at Nyasia's facial expression then back at Duevon's face like she was watching a ping pong match. She then rolled her eyes and grabbed the card and receipt from Nyasia's hand.

"You are so petty," Duevon laughed at her.

"I don't even understand what you are talking about," she played dumb and applied her Chanel lip gloss. "Yeah ok, because that felt a little like big bank take lil bank," he joked.

"Not at all, I'm appreciative of everything I have, and I hate that it took." She began before she let the rest of the sentence trail off.

"It took what?" Duevon pressed her.

"I don't want to talk about it," she turned cold on him suddenly. When the waitress returned with her card, Nyasia grabbed the card, and slid away from the table quickly. She then grabbed her purse and walked away from the table and out of the restaurant. He wasn't sure what he had done to offend her, but he wasn't letting her off the hook that easily.

"Nyasia," Duevon called out to her. She ignored him and continued to walk briskly towards her car. Running to catch up with her, he caught her right before she got inside.

"Why do you always shut down on me?" he questioned her angrily.

"I don't want to talk about it," she protested as tears filled her eyes.

"You can tell me anything. Is it another man? Do you date rich men to be able to afford this BMW, all of the designer purses, the expensive shoes, your condo, and some of these expensive restaurants we go to?" he asked her.

"Is that what you think? You think I'm a fucking prostitute?" she yelled loudly causing other people to look at them weirdly.

"I don't know what to think, because whenever we talk about you or things start to get too deep, you withdraw!" he yelled back at her.

"I'm not a damn prostitute! My parents died in a car crash five months ago. They had a large insurance policy. All of this material shit I have is because of them, but it means nothing without them," she cried as her heart tore into two. Unable to find the words to say, Duevon looked at her blankly. What she had just said was the last thing he was expecting. With her looks, her being with rich men was more believable than what she was saying. However, Duevon could tell by the way that she had completely come undone at the mention of her parents, that it was true. As he reminisced on their previous conversations, he realized that she didn't talk about her family much. She would listen to him complain about his mother for hours, but she would switch the topic whenever he asked about her relationship with her mother.

"I'm so sorry baby, I had no idea." Duevon told her as he tried to reach out to her.

"No, just leave me alone. I want to be alone!" She lashed out at him, while hitting the unlock button on her car. She then got into the car and sped away. Duevon wanted to go after her and console her, but he also wanted to give her space and let her come to him when she was ready. Walking over to his car, he jumped inside, placed his foot on the brake, and hit the push start to fire up the engine. As he drove to the condo that he had been subleasing, he began to imagine what his life would be life if he didn't have Stephanie. Sure, she was a bitch, she was always in his business, and she got on his last nerve; but she had loved him unconditionally all his life. She raised a child that someone else had given up. For that, she would always have his respect. It must have been hard having your parents all your life, then having them stripped away from you instantly. They knew what life had been like before their children, but children didn't know what life was like before their parents.

Pulling out his cellphone, he began to dial his mother number. Maybe he needed to be the bigger person and just talk things through with Stephanie. It was time that she accepted that he was a grown ass man that would date, fuck, and potentially marry a woman. She couldn't keep running every woman away from him because it was making him miserable. The phone rang, but she didn't answer it. Figuring that she probably still had an attitude because he hadnt reached out to her since his last game, he hung up the phone.

He decided to wait and call his mother again when he made it in the house safely. Turning his music up as loud as it would go, he zoned out and allowed muscle memory to take over and drive him home. Riding in the car, alone, with just the open road felt therapeutic. He began to think about Nyasia. She was filled with sadness, but she wore it well. No one would ever know that she had so much unhappiness inside of her. Her deep-seated scars exceeded his level, and he didn't know the first way to help her work through that trauma. His way of dealing with shit had been to suppress it and pretend that it didn't exist. It seemed as if his new friend was the same way. When Duevon made it to the luxury condo, overlooking the bayou, that he was renting from one of his teammates; he was surprised to find that he hadnt left a light on in the house. He had only been there for two weeks, so he was still getting used to the place. He fumbled around in the darkness trying to find the light switch, when suddenly a sharp pain went through his head.

Grabbing the back of his head, blows rang down on him from all different directions. He could tell by the various fists hitting him, and feet stomping him, that he had multiple attackers. He tried his hardest to fight back, but he didn't have any luck as they beat him mercilessly.

"HEEELPPPP!" he screamed out weakly as the beating felt like it was never ending.

"Flip his bitch ass over," one of the attackers said harshly as the group of men flipped him onto his back.

"Give me this chain bitch, I want the wallet to." One of the attackers said as the others continued to stomp him while one man took all of his shit.

Suddenly he felt steel as he realized that one of the men had pulled out a gun and began to beat him in the head with it.

"Asia is my hoe. You can't have her; it doesn't matter how much money you have." The man told him as he beat him in the head with the gun.

"See you in hell bitch." one of the men said as he cocked the gun sliding a bullet in the chamber. He then shot Devon twice in his right arm. It was his strongest arm, and the one he used the most. He was right-handed and could barely pick up a fork with his left hand.

"AAARGHHHH!" Devon grunted loudly as the bullets riddled his arm.

"That's enough nigga," one of the men told him harshly as he snatched the gun from the shooter and kicked Duevon again. The group of men then ran out of the door leaving it wide open. Laying defenseless, Duevon weakly tried to scream for help.

Realizing that he needed to help himself, he used all of

his strength to crawl over to his phone. The thieves had taken everything else but left his cell phone in the middle of the floor. Tears streamed down his face, as his arm went numb from all of the pain. Picking up the phone with his left hand, it slid from his hand easily. Determined, he reached for it again and shakily dialed the number that he was going to call less than thirty minutes ago.

"What the fuck do you want boy?" his mother answered the phone angrily.

"MAAAAAAA!" he screamed out to her like a child. She knew from his voice, that he was in serious trouble and serious pain.

"Oh my god baby, where are you? Tell me where you are mama's coming," she told him.

Unable to tell her where he was, he cried silently. This was Nyasia's fault. The story she had told him about her parent's and the little Oscar performance she had put on tonight was probably complete bullshit. Maybe she was fucking with niggas to finance the lifestyle she had. She had brought drama to his front door, that he never experienced fucking with another bitch. He prayed that he would be able to play football again as his head throbbed violently and he tried his best to keep consciousness. As a football player, he knew that going to sleep while he had a head injury was dangerous. He could slip into a coma if he had a concussion.

My mother was right about her. She's always right about these women he thought to himself as he laid on his injured arm and waited for his mother to come. The moonlight shone brightly into the window, and he could have sworn that he saw Kamya in a beautiful white dress looking down at him.

"I deserve this for what we did to you," he cried out to her painfully.

As he lay in agony, he reminisced on the worst day of his life.

Duevon had proposed to his high school sweetheart a few months after graduation. They had met their freshman year and dated for their four years of high school. He knew that she was the only woman for him. Originally from Bangladesh, Kamya was very religious, and she was taught that sex without marriage was a sin. Knowing that she was it for him, and he would never grow tired of her, Duevon snuck down to the courthouse with her and they secretly eloped. The night they got married was the best night of his life. They made sweet passionate love for the first time for hours. The very next day, his life changed forever. Kamya convince Duevon that they needed to tell his mother that they were married now. When they went to tell Stephanie the good news about their marriage, she pretended to be happy for them. The three of them sat around the dining room table, and Stephanie told them that she had an aged bottle of wine that was perfect for the occasion. Duevon was slightly surprised that she was taking the news so well, seeing as though she had been against their relationship from the very beginning. Nevertheless, he was naively excited that she was happy for them. A few seconds later, Stephanie returned to the dining room with a large butcher knife. She looked like a deranged killer as she smiled at them evilly. Kamya quickly jumped from the table and tried to run to the door to escape. She wasn't quick enough as Stephanie caught up to her and buried the nine-inch blade into her back. Screaming out in pain she fell to her knees. Ignoring her cries, Duevon watched in shock as his mother stabbed his 17-year-old wife repeatedly. He was too stunned to think. He was too stunned to speak. Watching Stephanie covered in blood as she continued to stab Kamya with no mercy was something out of a horror movie. He was expecting to wake up from the bad dream at any moment and be laying next to his wife. There was no way you could wake up if you weren't sleeping. This shit was real, and it was happening right in front of him. When his mother was done with her stabbing session, she walked to the kitchen. Finally able to find his strength Duevon tried to run to the door to get help. When he heard the sound of a bullet being released into the chamber, he froze like he was playing freeze tag.

"Going somewhere son?" she asked him maniacally.

Placing his hands up in surrender he turned around slowly to face her. She stood in the foyer holding a gun pointed at him with the bottle of wine and two wine glasses in her hand.

"Go sit down," she motioned with the gun causing him to run back over to the dining room table. Lowering the gun, she walked over, placed the bottle and two glasses on the table, and popped the top. She then began to pour both of them a glass as blood covered her hands and face. She sat in the seat his wife had once occupied and took a long sip of her drink before she began speaking.

"Either you help me bury this bitch or you go with her." Stephanie told him coldly as Kamya's body lay filled with stab wounds a few feet away.

Too afraid to go up against his mother, Duevon nodded sadly and averted his gaze downward. As beautiful as his mother had always been to him, he could see that her beauty was a façade. She was the devil in disguise. Raising her glass in the air he raised his as well, and they clinked glasses before both finishing their drink. In that moment, it felt as if he had made a deal with the devil. He helped her chop the body up and throw the pieces in a gator swamp and made up an elaborate story thatshe was tired of her parent's strict upbringing, so she ran away. No matter how much the authorities looked, they never found his wife. Since they didn't find a body, they couldn't definitely say that a crime had been committed. Torn up from the loss of their daughter, Kamya's family moved out of the country to put as much distance between themselves and the evil city of New Orleans, as they possibly could. With the right lawyer, Duevon was divorced quickly and quietly, and since they were both juveniles the records were sealed.

"I'm so sorry baby, I was a coward. I didn't stand up for you that day. I stood and watched her kill you and I could have done something about it." He cried out to the ghost of his dead wife as he felt his self-growing weaker. Adrenaline was fading from his body, so he was able to feel more pain. He could only see from one eye, so he assumed the other one was swollen shut. He could taste blood in his mouth that he felt draining from his nose, his lips were stinging so they had to be busted. His body ached all over like he had been in a terrible car accident. To keep himself sane he focused on his beautiful ex-wife. Indian and black, she had always been the most beautiful girl in the world to him. Suddenly her sweet angelic smile turned into a devilish grimace. Her once white dress was now covered in blood and all the stab wounds that Stephanie left behind marred her beauty. Unable to look at her, Duevon shut his eyes tight like a child that was avoiding the boogeyman. When he opened his eyes again, his mother was standing in front of him.

"What have they done to my baby? Who did this shit to you? I bet it had something to do with that girl, I told you she was going to bring you a world of heartache," his mother scolded him as she got on her knees and began to wipe the blood from his busted lip. Pulling out her cell phone, she dialed 911 then sat on the floor next to her baby. They cried together as they waited for the paramedics to arrive.

When Duevon was no longer able to hold on to consciousness he allowed the sleep to take over as he rested his eyes. "It's ok to sleep baby, mama's here," Stephanie murmured to him as he faded into oblivion.

Chapter Six

Nyasia threw her keys on the table when she made it inside of her apartment. She wiped her tears that were flowing freely, "A fucking prostitute," she said aloud to herself. As she walked past her mantel a beautiful picture of her parents sat in a crystal picture frame. "I miss you both so much," she rubbed the picture as she cried.

She had felt so alone in the world when they left her. That was until she met Duevon. Thinking of him her sadness turned to anger, he had a lot of nerve to try her the way he had. She couldn't believe she had opened up to him and told him her business. It was none of his concern where her money had come from. As far as she was concerned that was private. Even if he researched it, there was no way he would ever know that her parents had left her behind a large insurance policy if she hadn't opened her big mouth in the heat of the moment. Rolland her father's best friend, and their family lawyer had made her promise to never tell a soul that her parents had left her behind so much money. He knew that shit could get ugly, and people were getting killed and scammed left to right.

"Idiot, luckily you didn't tell the nigga how much you had with your big mouth ass; just stupid," she scolded herself as she went over to her wine pantry and poured a glass of red wine. What had started as a perfect dinner filled with laughter had turned into a complete nightmare. As one glass of wine turned into multiple, her anger with Duevon dissipated. As she sat at her table, alone, downing glasses of wine like they were H20, she began to realize that she had maybe overreacted. They had been dating for almost a month, and he had the right to be curious. She knew exactly how he made his money; he had no idea what she was into to afford her lifestyle. Prostitution was still alive and kicking in 2022.The majority of the social media models that had banging bodies and extravagant lifestyles were nothing but overpaid escorts. Everyone knew about it,but no one talked about it. What had she shown him to make him feel that she was any different? She never went to anyone's job, she wasn't in the entertainment industry. For all he knew, she probably made a living finessing rich men out of money. Could she really blame him for asking how she could afford a five-hundred-dollar restaurant tab?

One of the things she had learned from therapy was taking accountability. Feeling ashamed, she reached for her purse, so that she could get her cell phone and call him to apologize. When she finally dialed his number, it rang a few times. Before she could hang up the phone, a woman answered his phone.

"Don't call here anymore bitch," the woman told her harshly then ended the call in her face.

Looking at the phone as if an alien were about to come through it. She was shocked that it had taken no time for him to be in the next bitch's face. They hadn't been gone from each other for an hour yet.

"I know this nigga did not," she told herself as she tried to dial the number back to give him a piece of her mind. The phone went straight to voicemail as if her number had been blocked.

"I knew he wasn't shit," she shook her head. Duevon had really disappointed her and reminded her why she didn't date or give men a chance. To think that she had felt bad for the way she treated him and called to apologize. Picking her face up from the floor, she poured another glass of wine, and went to her master bathroom for a soak in her large jacuzzi tub. After a soul cleansing cry, and the rest of the bottle, she crawled into her California king bed and let the sleep take her away.

A light sleeper, Nyasia awoke to a small sound in the middle of the night. Opening her eyes, she moved slightly to see if the sound would be repeated. She didn't hear anything. Dismissing it as paranoia, she turned over on her side. Suddenly, she heard the low sound again. Leaning over to her nightstand, she pulled the drawer out quietly and reached for her chrome plated 32. As a woman living alone, she couldn't be too careful and just pepper spray wasn't enough Grabbing the gun, she silently slipped out of bed and crept behind her bedroom door. Her phone was in her purse on the other side of the room, and she didn't think she could creep over to it to call the police.

How the fuck did they get in? she thought to herself as her heart raced. Her hands shook nervously, and she had never been more terrified in her life

"Be quiet nigga you are loud as fuck." One of the men told the other as they walked through her house.

When their footsteps began to grow closer to her room, she clicked the safety off the gun. This was her first time shooting someone, but she had to do what she had to do. If it came down to her life or theirs, she was definitely choosing herself. The door was wide open, and two men walked into her room. They were both large in size, tall, and dressed in all black. She pushed herself further into the wall as she prayed that they wouldn't turn around and see her.

"Is she here?" one of the men whispered.

"Her car is parked out front, where else could she be?" the other man asked.

"Maybe she called an uberand left. Hell, she could be anywhere." He replied angrily.

"Well, we did what we came to do. Let's go," he replied as he turned around to walk out the door. The moment he turned around, he noticed her standing behind her door. Without thinking she lifted her gun and began to shoot.

"SHIT!" he screamed out as the bullet pierced his arm. Not

sure where she was aiming, she continued to fire as he ran past her and out of the room. Turning to follow them, she fired her gun. Her first shot had to be a lucky one. As the men ran away, she hit her large tv, one of her crystal vases, and the wall. She needed to go to the gun range and get some practice. She may have been a a terrible shot, but the men were running away so that was good enough for her. When they ran out of the door. She slammed it behind them, locked it, and ran to her phone to dial 911. Frantically, she called the police and explained that two men had broken into her house. She couldn't describe them because they were wearing all black, with ski masks, and it was dark in her home.

Ten minutes later the police arrived, since the assailants were gone, the only thing they could do was make a report. Feeling unsafe, she decided to catch an uber and go to a hotel room for the night. They knew what she was driving, and they had come into her house to do something, but she had no idea what they had come to do. Were they coming to rape her? Kill her? Rob her? She hadn't made any enemies since she had been here besides Duevon's mother. When she was safely tucked away in the hotel, she pulled out here phone and attempted to call him again. The same thing happened; her call went straight to voicemail. Did he have something to do with the two men trying to rob her since he now knew that she had received an inheritance from her parents? Life was so crazy, there was just no way of knowing a person's real intentions. She cried herself to sleep as she wished that her parents were there to help her navigate the murky waters of dating in your twenties. For the first time since she picked up and left Atlanta, she began to feel that her friends were right about moving to another city completely alone. She had never been through anything like this in her hometown.

"You were right about everything mama. Nyasia is nothing but a scheming gold digger. She convinces me to let my guard down and trust her, then some nigga that she fucks with, and his broke ass friends rob me for thousands of dollars' worth of jewelry and jump me." Duevon told his mother the next day as he laid in the hospital bed bandaged up.

"Now son, I don't like the little bitch either, but what makes you so sure she had something to do with this?" his mother questioned as she held the Jell-O cup in her hand and fed it to him in small spoonful's. The doctors had completed their tests and by the grace of God, he didn't have a concussion, or any major physical damage besides the gun shots to his arm. The bullets hadn't hit any major arteries. After a few months of physical therapy, he would be back to new. The problem was he would have to sit his last few games of the season out, and that would take a large chunk of his salary. That pissed him off and he was seeing red.

"HE TOLD ME!" The nigga stopped beating me to say, "leave Nyasia alone, that's my bitch," Duevon told his mother angrily causing her to gasp in surprise.

"That little bitch, I'm going to snatch her throat out for fucking with my baby! I told you she couldn't be trusted," his mother replied angrily.

"I thought she was different mom. You were right, the only woman I can trust is you. These bitches are all the same. When they see me, they just see a check," he told her sadly as tears filled his eyes. He was heartbroken because he was just about to ask her to officially be his woman. Even though they hadn't fucked yet, he had fallen for her.

"Dry your fucking eyes Duevon! I didn't raise a bitch so don't you dare cry over this girl. If you don't want me to make her pay, at least let me call the police. You said your shit was stolen, we are going to file a report and they will get all of your things back from that low life skank. She is not going to get away with this and run off into the sunset," his mother told him as she pulled her cell phone from her pocket. Twenty minutes later, Duevon was talking to a detective and filing a report against Nyasia.

"We need a restraining order as well; I don't want that bitch within twenty feet of my son." Stephanie told the detective angrily as she paced back and forth.

"Would you like a restraining order Mr. Howell?" the detective asked him with one eyebrow raised. With twenty years on the force, he had seen these types of situations where young love turned violent. The men didn't want to leave their little crazy girlfriend's alone until someone ended up in jail or in a body bag.

"Yes officer, I would like a restraining order against her, and I want to press charges," Duevon replied sadly.

"Good, it's the right thing to do. I saw your last game, and you are an extremely talented young man. Don't let a young lady ruin your future, there will be plenty more down the line," the detective schooled him as if he were his own son. "Your mother is right about this so listen to her, like they say Mother's know best!" he told Duevon as he wrote on his notepad. After Duevon described all of his items that were taken, the detective called in a search warrant for Nyasia's home to see if any of the items were there. If they found any of his items that were missing, it would be proof to back up his claims and they could start legal proceedings against the young woman.

"Ok, I have a search warrant. I am headed to the courthouse to pick it up and then after that I will go over to her house to see if we can locate your things. Do me a favor and do not reach out to her or contact her anymore after today if you are serious about taking legal action against her. It could ruin your entire case," the detective told him as he closed up his notepad and walked out of the door.

Feeling like a fool, Duevon let his mother feed him the rest of the Jell-O and give him orange juice as the nurse came in with another round of pain killers. The strong meds eased him into a deep slumber. He dreamed about the beautiful future he could have had with Nyasia if she hadn't betrayed him.

Waiting until Duevon was sound asleep, Stephanie stepped out of the hospital room and into the hallway. She walked towards the women's bathroom, while reaching for her cell phone. When she finally made it inside, she opened the door to each stall to make sure that she was alone. After that, she went over to the door and locked it before making her call.

"Yes, Boss lady?" the security guard who had escorted her out of Caesars Superdome a few weeks earlier answered the call. Since the day she had paid them to release her, she now had both bouncers on her payroll. They had been watching both Nyasia and Duevon for her and reporting their whereabouts.

"Which one of you motherfuckers broke my son's nose and blacked his eye?" she questioned them angrily.

She had made specific instructions that they were to steer clear of his face at all times. He was too handsome to be laid up in a bed with a busted lip, a broken nose, and a black eye. They would have to see her about fucking up her son's face. She didn't know why she had expected a couple of niggas with a third-grade education between the both of them, to be able to comprehend and follow simple instructions. She had told them to shoot him twice in the arm, kick his ass, but avoid his face.

"Uhh Um," the man stuttered terribly.

"Speak up motherfucker," she demanded as she slapped her open palm on the porcelain bathroom sink.

"It was one of the niggas we hired boss lady. He's new and it was his first time. I know you said that you wanted it to be a large group of us so Duevon wouldn't remember us from the stadium, so I had to improvise with my recruiting," he finally found his voice and answered her.

"Improvise huh? Well, how would you feel if I improvise with paying your dumb ass?" she questioned him angrily.

"I'm sorry boss lady. I will make it up to you. We.... We did everything else you asked. We planted some of Duevon's jewelry in Nyasia's apartment and scared that bitch to death," he laughed shyly.

Stephanie smiled sinisterly. She would have paid any amount to see the tough bitch with all the mouth fold when her two men broke into her apartment. These bitches were so tough until you actually pulled their card to see where their heart was.

"When will you be able to pay us the money?" he questioned her.

"As soon as the little bitch gets arrested so I can know you did your part correctly, you will get your money. Pleasure doing business with you gentleman," she dismissed him and ended the call in his face. Looking in the mirror, she fixed her hair and blew a kiss at her reflection. She knew that if she wanted to hit Duevon where it hurt, she had to take the one thing he loved more than everything including her; Football. Sitting the rest of the season out would be punishment for him making a mockery of her at the game. He was still young, so he would heal up nicely and be back in the game next season like he never left. Also, she knew that her son was right-handed. If she took away his ability to take care of himself, he would have no choice but to need her. He was about to give up that funky ass apartment and move back into the mansion with her the minute he was released from the hospital. She had missed having her baby boy right down the hallway. He would be right back where he belonged close enough where she could keep her eyes on him. He wasn't ready for the world; he still needed her even if he didn't think he did.

Chapter Seven

When Nyasia returned to her house the next day, the daylight made her feel safer, but she still felt like a stranger in her own home. She had left everything exactly as it was, so the place was a mess. The bullet was still lodged in her fifty-inch flatscreen television, the glass from the crystal vase lay all over the floor and the water had soaked into her Persian rug. Putting her purse on the table but being sure that her 32 was on her hip and her cell phone was in her pocket, Nyasia began to clean up the mess. She had finally swept up the glass, picked the rug up, placed it over the shower rail to dry, as well as began to dig the bullet holes out of the walls when there was a loud bang on her door. Still startled from the night before, she jumped out of her skin at the noise.

"It's just the door scary ass," she told herself as she stood from her knees and walked over to open the door. She was shocked to find a man in a suit with two police officers behind him.

Maybe they are coming to get another statement about what happened from last night, she thought to herself.

Hell, maybe they caught the niggas that broke in my house because I know I hit one of their asses, she also thought to herself.

"Nyasia Banks?" The officer in the front spoke while the other two just stood and looked at her like shit on the bottom of their shoe. She could see why people preferred street justice over getting the police involved in their business. She had been the victim, and they were standing there giving her nasty looks like she had done the damn crime.

"Yes, that's me officer. How can I help you?" she asked him

snidely.

"I'm Detective Jackson and received a report from a Mr. Duevon Howell that you had him set up to be robbed and assaulted last night. Before you say anything, I have a detailed account of everything that is missing, and I have a search warrant to enter the premises," the detective told her rudely.

Her mouth fell open, and there was nothing she could say or do aside from look at him blankly.

"What do you mean robbed and assaulted? Where is Duevon? Is he ok? I haven't laid eyes on him since we had dinner yesterday around 6pm. I assumed you came to follow up on the two men that broke into my house last night. I have a police report and I shot one of them. There was no way I could have been breaking into his home while someone was breaking into mine," she protested.

"Step aside ma'am," the detective pushed past her like she didn't mean anything and began to search her house.

"This is the second time in twenty-four hours that some niggas have busted up in my house without permission. Get the hell out of here!" Nyasia yelled.

"Ma'am if you interfere with an ongoing investigation, whether we find something or not, you will be arrested. Your best bet will be to go over there, sit down, and let us look around the place. We have the legal right to be here." The detective dismissed her then proceeded to fuck up the house she had just worked so hard to clean.

Grabbing her cell phone, Nyasia picked up her phone and called her lawyer. More and more this town was bringing her more drama than it was worth, and she was ready to put a for sale sign on her condo and take her ass back to Atlanta. It seemed like everywhere she turned she was getting attacked, and she was a strong believer in signs. When it was time for you to get out of a certain situation, life would begin to get uncomfortable. Right now, discomfort was an understatement for what she was feeling as she watched the police officers rip her home apart that she had spent so much money to decorate. They had little regard for treating her shit delicately even though a few of those figurines costed more than they probably made in a year.

"This is a really nice place you have here Ms. Banks, what do you do for a living?" The detective asked her while smirking. She could tell that he was being funny and one of those asshole cops that didn't have a life outside of work. He probably hasn't had a piece of pussy in decades with his cheap polyester suit.

"Nothing I care to share," she dismissed him while continuing to talk to her lawyer on the phone.

"I have a buddy in New Orleans that I can call to sort this shit out right now, but I'm on the next flight down just hang tight Asia," Rolland told her lovingly. Tears filled her eyes as she thought about the last time, she had heard her father call her that. It was the day that he died. He was on his way to meet her mother for their weekly dinner at their favorite restaurant. She had called to remind him to grab her a doggy bag from the restaurant because she was in the middle of studying for a huge test in Geology. They laughed and talked as he drove and the last thing he said to her, before he ended the call, was I love you Asia. Nyasia had replayed that conversation in her head at least once a day, every day since his death.

"Please be sure to get here quickly because I'm feeling harassed. I'm the fucking victim. My home was burglarized last night, and all New Orleans PD did was write some shit on a piece of paper, and hand it to me. The very next day, they are accusing me of something, and they have all the time in the world to tear my house apart," Nyasia stated angrily.

"Don't worry, this shit will be over by dinner. They obviously have no idea who you are or who you have behind you. See you shortly," her lawyer told her.

"I hope that was your lawyer Ms. Banks because I'm going

to have to take you down to the station for questioning," the detective told her while smiling and holding Duevon's bloody chain in his gloved hand. It was the same necklace that he had been wearing the night before while they were at dinner. She hadn't laid eyes on him or that chain since she left him at the restaurant.

"This is some type of mistake, Duevon hasn't been here. I don't know how the hell that got here," Nyasia protested as one of the officers walked up to her and placed her hands behind her back. "I suggest you don't say another word young lady. You are only further incriminating yourself," the detective replied as he placed the necklace and some other jewelry in a plastic zip loc bag. The things were colored in blood like they had been lying in a murder scene and it made her sick to her stomach.

They escorted her out of her home like she was nothing more than a common criminal as nosey people stood around and watched in disgust.

Nyasia waived her right to questioning without a lawyer present and sat in the jail cell for an hour before she was released on bond.

"How are you Ms. Banks? My name is Michael Strain and I'm here on behalf of your lawyer Rolland," the handsome white attorney introduced himself when she walked out of the building.

"Nice to meet you Michael, thank you for your help back there." She nodded at the building behind her as she tried to put as much distance between herself and the detention center as possible. She didn't know how her lawyers had gotten her out so quickly, but she was glad to be free. That was her first and last time in someone's dirty jail.

"For a special client like yourself, no problem at all. The judge wants a hearing first thing in the morning. Rolland's flight lands in a few hours, but I will still be there to assist. It seems like you have pissed some pretty powerful people off Ms. Banks," Michael shook his head at her. "I dated the wrong football player," she shrugged as she walked over to his car.

When they finally made it to her door, she went inside and grabbed another spend a night bag. She wasn't staying here in this home that they had ripped apart when she had just made it decent again. She was going back to the hotel for the night. Getting into her car, she started the car and drove a few miles down the road before she heard a large clanking sound and it cut off on her in the middle of the street.

"NOT AGAIN JESUS," she banged on the steering wheel and steered the car over into a parking lot. Luckily, she hadn't been in the middle of traffic when her car shut off because she would have caused a ten-car pileup. Getting out the car, she assumed it was another flat tire. After walking around the car, she kicked each tire but there was no glass, nail, or sharp object in sight. They were in perfect condition. She suddenly noticed a thin cloud of smoke coming from her gas tank. She opened it, and it was filled with white powder. Someone had put sugar in her gas tank and blew the engine to her car that she had gotten only a few short months ago.

"I'M GETTING THE FUCK OUT OF THIS CITY!" she screamed to the top of her lungs as she stomped her feet in aggravation.

She called a tow truck to take the car back to her address, then called an Uber to take her to the hotel. This day had been shitty for her, and she simply wanted tomorrow to come. The sooner she could get this shit worked out with Duevon's jewelry being in her house, the quicker she could get the hell out of New Orleans Louisiana.

Rolland called her first thing the next morning, so she could meet him at Café Du Monde before they had to meet with the judge at the courthouse downtown. She had gone by her house, changed clothes, then headed right back out in lightning speed. As she sat across the table from him, she sipped her coffee and told him everything. She began with how she and Duevon had initially met and concluded on the last time they spoke. She even told him about her huge fight with Duevon's mother Stephanie at the game.

Rolland listened intently, then pulled out a manilla folder and slid it to her.

"What is this?" she asked him nervously as she opened the folder to see what was inside.

"This is everything I was able to dig up on Duevon since I have been here. These records were sealed so there was no way you would have ever found out if he didn't tell you. Fortunately, everything and everyone has a price," he told her while sipping his coffee.

As Nyasia went through the folder, tears filled her eyes as she read about the case of Duevon and Kamya. Out of all the conversations he had with her, he neglected to mention that he was married seven years ago. "He didn't tell me anything about this!" Nyasia exclaimed as she read through the notes.

"Of course, he didn't, they were married for one day. They checked into a room at this hotel, staff saw them leave together the very next day, and this young lady was never heard from again. The case was fishy even to the police, but a lot of times knowing the right people at the right time can get you out of some sticky situations. This guy is bad news Nyasia and I'm just glad that you were able to get out of this situation, before some weird shit happened to you that nobody could explain" Rolland told her. Nodding her head and taking a huge gulp, Nyasia finished her coffee and beignets in silence.

Thirty minutes later, she was waiting patiently in the judge's chambers for the small hearing to begin. Both Rolland and Michael were sitting next to her, the detective that had arrested her yesterday sat across from her, the bailiff stood near the door, and the pale faced judge sat sweaty behind his desk as he taped his foot nervously.

"Was the victim and his counsel notified of the hearing time, they are only a few minutes from being late and you know how important punctuality is in my courtroom. My time is not to be played with," the judge glared at the detective. A few seconds later, the door opened and in walked Stephanie, a tall man with thick rimmed glasses, and Duevon.

When Nyasia laid eyes on him, she gasped in shock at how terrible he looked.

"Oh my God Duevon," she said as she stood to her feet and was about to walk over to him.

"Control your client," the judge told Rolland and he grabbed Nyasia by her elbow and pulled her back to her seat. "You have some type of nerve, trying to act all concerned when you did this to him. My baby can't even finish the season because of you." Stephanie gritted her teeth and Duevon flashed Nyasia a look that could melt ice.

"Same goes for you counselor, I know emotions are high behind this issue, but I need you to control your client!" the judge turned to Stephanie's lawyer.

"I'm straight," Stephanie snapped on her lawyer before he could say anything. She then walked over to the chair, pulled it out for Duevon as he limped to his seat, she then helped him as he sat down.

The bitch might as well pull out her titty and breast feed him while she's at, Nyasia thought to herself in annoyance. Her heart had told her that all of this shit was Stephanie's doing. Duevon's attack, her home invasion, the bloody evidence in her house all feltlike a ploy to keep the baby boy in the nest. If Duevon didn't see through the things his mother did now, he never would.

Today was October 31st and this was not how she had envisioned spending her Halloween, but life rarely went as planned.

"Sorry we are late your honor, but because of my clients' substantial injuries it was difficult to get him down here. When he leaves, he is returning to the hospital for more tests to be sure that his injuries won't generate any future health issues for him," the lawyer exaggerated Duevon's health to get the judge to pity him. It was his job to paint Duevon out to be the victim, and to paint Nyasia to be the evil perpetrator.

As the hearing went on, the judge listened intensely to both sides of the story. For every time Stephanie's lawyer tried to throw a jab at Nyasia, her lawyers threw two right hooks in return. Nyasia and Duevon had been dating, so it wasn't farfetched that a piece of his jewelry could be in her house. The only leg they had to stand on was the fact that the jewelry was found covered in Duevon's blood and it was one of the items he listed that had been taken from him. With no solid evidence connecting Nyasia to the crime, and her verifiable reports that she had also been assaulted on the same night, both parties came to a mutual agreement. If Nyasia signed a non-disclosure agreement about the case so she wouldn't tarnish Duevon's reputation, and if she agreed to a mandatory restraining order, the judge would dismiss the case and all charges against her would be dropped. She would be free, and this shit would all be behind her. She couldn't sign the paperwork fast enough, as Duevon stared at her in disgust. After their lawyers shook hands, Nyasia walked out of the room with her head held high.

"If you are going to stay here, please steer clear of those two. They both give me fucked up vibes and I don't trust either of them as far as I can throw them," Rolland told her as she walked him to his Uber. He had a red eye flight back to Atlanta departing in less than an hour. He had to make it to Louis Armstrong International Airport so he could make it through security. He had come and handled business, he was now headed back home to his wife and children.

"I'm on the first flight out of here in the morning, I promise," Nyasia told him as she hugged him tightly. If it hadn't been for him, the Howells would have planted some bullshit on her, and she would be still sitting in jail right now behind something she had nothing to do with.

"Take care of my girl," he told Michael as he opened the car door and got inside.

"I've got her" Michael replied as he waved at Rolland

When the car was out of sight, Michael spoke. "Would you like to have dinner with me and my family tonight? I have extra rooms and my home is yours. Any friend of Rolland's is a friend of mine," the attorney offered.

Half of her wanted to take him up on his offer. She didn't want to be alone in this eerie ass city, with two people that hated her guts for no good reason. The other half of her didn't want to be looked at as some stranger or a charity case that Michael had brought home like a stray dog. She only needed to make it through one more night here and New Orleans would never see her again.

"As amazing as that sounds I have to decline. Thank you so much for all of your help, but I'm leaving tomorrow, and I have a lot to do. I need to go back to my apartment and pack somethings to take with me since I have nothing in Atlanta, I also need to get some quotes on moving companies, book my flight, find a realtor to put my place on the market, there's just so much to do," she shook her head in defeat.

"One step at a time. Take my phone number, and here is my address in case you change your mind about coming over. You have had a tough time over the past few days, so don't be so hard on yourself. I'm here to help in any way I can." Michael told her as he rubbed her back.

He waited with her until her Uber arrived to take her back to her hotel room, he then got into his Audi and pulled away. When she made it to the room, she ordered room service, booked her flight to Atlanta, and began to research moving companies and relators. Even though it was Halloween, it was still Monday so a lot of businesses were up and running like usual. She was able to lock in a phenomenal quote with a moving company and had an appointment to speak with the highest rated realtor in New Orleans at the end of the week. All she needed to do, was go back to her house, pack up, and get the hell out of there quickly.

After court, Duevon was in a sour mood and Stephanie could tell. She had tried to crack jokes and he didn't laugh at any of them, she had offered to cook for him when they made it home, and he reluctantly agreed. He had withdrawn, and was dealing with extreme sadness. He couldn't finish the rest of the season, it was hard to sit across from a woman he cared about and not talk to her or hug her, and hehe had ended up right back where he started. He was in his room, down the hall from his mother like a prisoner. When Stephanie knocked on his door, he was laying in his bed looking up at the ceiling.

"Hey baby, I'm sorry that you are going through this, do you want me to give you some meds?" she asked him. She felt that if he was sleeping, she wouldn't have to worry about him while she went to the supermarket to pick up dinner, she knew her famous lasagna would lift his spirits.

"Yeah, my arm is killing me," Duevon complained. She smiled and walked up to him with the meds and a bottle of water in her hand.

'Thank you so much mom. I can always count on you." Duevon told her as he took the pill and gulped down the entire bottle of water.

"Get some rest, I'm going to the store to get some dinner," she told him sweetly before walking out of his room.

Thirty minutes later, he snored loudly while waiting for her to leave out the door. When he heard her loud footsteps enter his room, then come closer to his bed, he kept his eyes closed and pretended to be sleeping. He could hear her coming closer to him, as if she was making sure that he was really asleep. He focused on his breathing so she wouldn't suspect that he was faking. He wished he had another set of eyes to figure out why the hell she hadn't walked out of the room already. Suddenly, Duevon felt her warm lips on his as she kissed him passionately. He felt sick to his stomach as he counted down the seconds until she was done.

"We are all we have and all we need." Stephanie whispered in his ear before she walked out of his bedroom door.

He wondered how many times she had done that to him in the past when he was actually sleeping as he wiped his lips with the back of his hands. He got out of the bed, and slipped on a pair of sweatpants, a jacket, and some shoes. He struggled to get dressed with his dominant hand being in a sling, but he managed. He then went searching for his cell phone, he found it in the hospital bag with his things. He was getting the hell out of there before his mother tried to fuck him next. He didn't know what came over her, but this was the final straw for him. Even though he was injured, he was leaving this house and getting the hell away from her. As he packed a bag of clothes, he called Nyasia.

When he dialed her number, the phone rang a few times, and he heard the phone answer. She didn't say anything, but she was holding the phone because he could hear her breathing.

"Just tell me that you didn't do that shit Nyasia?" he asked her angrily.

"Are you going to believe me?" she asked him.

"Don't answer my question with a question! I went up against my mother for you and you turned right around and proved her right," Duevon told her angrily.

"Duevon, I know you aren't the brightest tool in the box, so I'm going to lay some shit on the line for you. I hope that it registers. The last time you saw or spoke with your mother, you and she had a huge fight. A few weeks later you are attacked, robbed, and two niggas break into my house. The next day, my ass gets hauled to jail for setting you up because the police find your bloody jewelry in my house. Plus, someone poured sugar in the tank of my car. Whether you want to accept it or not, your mother is behind all of this shit." Nyasia told him angrily

Speechless, Duevon wanted to tell her that she sounded crazy, but he couldn't. His mind flashed back to when she pulled the gun on him when he tried to get Kamya help. If Stephanie thought he was choosing another woman over her, there was no telling what she would do. Plus, he hadnt remembered telling his mother where he lived, but somehow, when he called, she knew exactly where to come.

"What do you mean again?" he questioned as he avoided making a comment about what Nyasia had just said. In a true man's fashion, he had looked over her entire rant and went for the most significant part to respond to.

"I know you were married before. I also know that your wife went missing and was never heard from again the day after yall were married. You can play dumb all you want, but for future references you need to warn bitches before you start fucking with them. You are attached to a crazy ass woman that would do anything to keep you to herself. Unlike the issue with most men, the crazy woman isn't your wife, an ex, or a bitter baby mother, IT'S YOUR FUCKING MAMA. You and her should just fuck and be together. Goodbye Duevon, lose my number." Nyasia ended the call in his face.

Duevon had called her in the middle of packing her shit and, she hastily threw the rest of the stuff in the bag. Calling an uber to take her back to her room, she slept with one eye open as she counted down the hours until she was on a plane out of New Orleans and headed home.

The next day, Nyasia was in route to Hartsfield Jackson Airport. She sat in first class, sipped a glass of champagne, and used her laptop to enroll into Georgia State University for Spring semester. This year had taken a lot out of her, but she knew that she was stronger than she had always believed she was. It was time to get back on the horse and create a life for herself that her parents would be proud of. Besides, it was the first of November, and if she could survive Halloween in New Orleans with A Mama's boy, she could survive a few more semesters of college...

THE END

T'ANN MARIE PRESENTS: GRANDMA'S HOUSE | Facebook

T'ANN MARIE PRESENTS: GRANDMA'S HOUSE 2.0 | Facebook

WIN PRIZES, BE APART OF LIVE BOOK DISCUSSIONS & MORE!

Join Our Mailing List:

http://eepurl.com/gU81k5